# Of Going Forth By Day

For Julia

# Of Going Forth By Day

Osiris, illustration by A.B.Cromar after Papyrus of Ani

# Matthew Stringer

© Matthew Stringer 2020

ISBN 9798690359256

# Contents

Introduction      vii

Inferno      1

     Ravenna, 1983      3

     Old Aberdeen, 1914      12

     Interzone      20

     Bologna, 1910      26

Purgatorio      31

     Rothiemurchus Forest, summer 2020      33

     In Garbh Coire      37

     Beneath Crown Buttress      42

     The Earthly Paradise      46

Paradiso      49

     Aberdeen, 2020      51

Endnotes      55

# Introduction

Following the death of George Lewis Quain in February of this year, I published several of the finds made in his library over the following fourteen or so weeks. *The Song of the Pirate Queen* was first, later that same month. Four further works followed by early June. The speed with which these were prepared and issued was aided by the imposition from mid-March of the restrictions to control the spread of the Covid-19 coronavirus, there being far fewer alternative uses of time to distract me from that task than would ordinarily have been the case. As for so many others, my office-based employment became working from home. Sitting at my own computer, connecting remotely to office networks, videoconferencing with colleagues, I discovered just how much I missed the ordinary human interaction of the office routine, how poor a substitute the technology offered. And all other socialising was curtailed as well. Dealing with the contents of Quain's library gave me a focus and purpose during those first few months of lockdown.

In time, however, isolation took its psychological toll. The pandemic has been a peculiarly lethargic catastrophe for many, and I found myself among that number. I was aware of the advice to try to maintain routine, to attempt to separate work from home, to dress properly for the former despite it being conducted in a room a yard across the hallway from my bedroom. Others perhaps did better in practice, though.

The most obvious physical evidence of my deterioration was in the condition of the hair of my face and head as displayed each day in the bathroom mirror. Hirsute became unkempt became untidy became wild. This change seemed to me to parallel those in the literary materials with which I was dealing: the whimsy of *The Song of the Pirate Queen* and *A Letter for Maggie Cromar* had given way to the difficulties of *The Lost Letters of Cardinal Bessarion*; *The Properties of Wool* I had then assembled with the inclusion of some materials of my own following from my interactions with George Lewis Quain; then there had been the awful hidden crime and disguised identities of *The Fate of the Farquharsons*. The anthropophagic theme had then been revisited, apparently now from the hand of the still-anonymous poet of *The*

*Song of the Pirate Queen*, in *An Island Cookbook*. This, however, did not represent an end to the materials.

I discovered an account by Dr. Alexander Blaikie Cromar of a conversation between himself and that same academic to whom Beatrice Innes had given the false name Professor Farquharson, and then, too, one of another conversation, this time between Dr. Cromar and one Francesco Atti, owner of a bookshop in Bologna. It seemed that this latter was the meeting in 1910 from which the Doctor had brought away not only the collection of letters of Cardinal Bessarion, but also those books listed by Diana Cromar in *The Fate of the Farquharsons* as having been given to the Professor after the death of her father.

In addition to these accounts by Dr. Cromar there was, under the heading '*Inferno*', what initially appeared to be an account by George Lewis Quain of a holiday to Ravenna in the spring of 1983. Parallels to the opening cantos of Dante's *Divine Comedy* were apparent: whether these were extruded from real experiences or evidence of a fiction was initially unclear. As I went on, however, it quickly became obvious that I was not dealing with a straightforward journal of Quain's travels: a collection of authors, all American (all but one from the United States), thinly disguised as their own literary creations, were met in circumstances at odds with their own biographies, before the account slid beyond magical realism into the fantastical. First time and then place ceased to cohere, with the final section being in a form I initially took to be mere notes, jotted ideas perhaps later to be turned into prose. On further consideration I revised this view, suspecting that it might be a stylistic choice and an allusion to the work of an additional American writer of special relevance to the Dantesque theme. My thoughts on these issues are covered at some length in my endnotes, which I hope should guide the reader through the depths of this section's literary torments, although my speculations are necessarily more tentative than definitive.

Then, at half past seven in the morning of the ninety-ninth day of lockdown, I walked into my bathroom and looked into the mirror, expecting to see myself reflected (albeit this recently re-wilded version of myself) but was faced instead by some stranger, some other, staring rudely back at me with no allowance for personal space.

It was not that he didn't look like me. I was well aware of the savage state of my facial hair, having seen myself in that same mirror just the day before: I knew that I looked just like this stranger. In addition, he obediently copied my movements to the last detail. But he was not me. I could see it in his eyes. He was an imposter, some *doppelgänger* (the Germans, as is their way, having a word for it) who had invaded the virtual world beyond the mirror, usurping the place of my reflection. He ran his fingers (his left, copying my right) through the unkempt beard twining from his cheek, keeping perfect time with my lead, and then retreated leftward out of sight as I moved to my right to leave the bathroom.

From that moment the bathroom was a place of fear for me, the mirror having become monstrous. Although the other who inhabited it looked as scared as me, and, as far as I could tell, limited himself only to slavishly copying my own movements in exact, if stereoisomeric, detail, I suspected him of malicious intent. He was, after all, somehow aware of my movements when I could not see him, constantly monitoring, constantly ready to step into my field of view and commence his mocking mimicry.

There is in my living room another mirror. It hangs above the fireplace, set in an art nouveau wooden frame. It is too high up to show me my reflection when sat on the sofa, as one usually is in that room, so I had forgotten it, but now I went, filled with trepidation, consciously to look into it and see who looked back. I saw immediately that this second mirror had also stopped showing me simply my own reflection through the straightforward properties of optics, but rather was occupied by the *doppelgänger* instead, just as the one in the bathroom. I sought him out elsewhere: faint in the glass doors of a cabinet or the pane of a picture-frame; deformed or inverted in the curvature of a spoon. I couldn't fathom the geometry of that other world as indicated by these windows: even allowing for an architecture by Maurits Escher, it evaded my desperately grasping mind.

I wondered how it was that I knew with such certainty that this was not my reflection who was looking at me. I considered in what had consisted my previous certainty that the person in the mirror was me. I had no clear answer. Obviously they could not actually be me: I was the one in here, 'this' rather than the 'that' beyond the plane of the mirror. I recalled the optical explanation. Something nagged me about it, some tiny thread hanging out of place in the grand tapestry of the scientific paradigm. I tugged at it.

I had, I saw, previously accepted the idea that I was not alone in the world. Of course there were other people out there: despite the lockdown I still occasionally had to visit a supermarket, and there they all still were, although slower and quieter than they had been a few months previously. But whereas before I had taken it for granted that they had internal lives, equivalent to the consciousness I experienced as myself, now I began to doubt: to see them as mere meat machines, philosophical zombies only simulating conscious beings. We kept our distance from each other, talking as little as we could, and that through the muffling inconvenience of face masks. What was the distinction between these quiet, distant creatures and my double who inhabited that convoluted world on the far side of the mirror-pane? Why should I ascribe an inner life to the former but deny it in the latter? The distinction was unclear.

I came to feel that the man in the mirror showed me more signs of conscious awareness. He was more attentive for one thing. But I had been given no cause to judge my double a greater threat than those others outdoors. Rather than this leading me to trust him more, though, I found myself progressively less trusting of the supermarket staff and fellow customers in the outside world.

I recognised through all this that these modified perspectives had come about in consequence of my isolation from more usual levels of social interaction. But it did not follow that my new notions were less correct than my previous delusions, however long I had been subject to them: it was precisely their extended, immersive constancy which had habituated me to them, rather than any conclusively superior evidence.

Over the following weeks the limitations of Descartes' maxim, *cogito ergo sum,* were also reached: without the mirror of others to whom to express them, my ideas lost form, and I slowly ceased from coherent thought. I needed linguistic communication to hold together my mind, and, therefore, my being. Both television and the internet made a noise which resembled language, but, I found, contained no evidence of being the expression of conscious human thought. I had suspected so before, but it was depressing that this, among all my previous delusions, appeared to be solid fact.

My response to the situation in which I found myself was to run away. Once lockdown restrictions were partially lifted, but while social distancing measures were still enforced, I fled to the wilds as a means to escape the tyranny of mirrors and my pursuit by the one who inhabited them. Despite predictions of thunderstorms I headed for the Cairngorms, this in itself perhaps evidence of shortcomings in my mental state at the time.

That I am writing this testifies to my survival. Indeed it is probably the case that I benefited psychologically from the experience, although my recollection of it includes an episode which reason urges me to disbelieve. I recorded my experiences in the mountains as I remembered them.

At this a thin ray which lit my hope shone from the materials taken from the library of the late George Lewis Quain. The character of my account of the experience in the Cairngorms fitted, I saw, with the mythological subject matter of of the discussions recorded by Dr. Cromar and also the fantastical intrusion of the literary into the real of the account of George Lewis Quain. I returned to his strange travelogue, divided it, and interleaved with it the mythological musings of Dr. Cromar in discussion with, firstly, Professor Farquharson and, secondly, Signor Atti. Having done so, I saw that my own mountain adventures could reasonably form a continuation of Quain's *Inferno*, being a parallel climbing out of Hell towards Heaven corresponding to Dante's *Purgatorio*. To these I appended some subject matter relevant to my recovery from my torments, located obviously in The Earthly Paradise which is the last stage of Purgatory, before a conclusion under the title of *Paradiso*.

In this way I forced meaning onto my own experiences and structure onto the fragmentary writings of both Quain and Dr. Cromar. It may be argued that I have done violence to their original intentions in subordinating their work to my own purpose, which is a charge I shall not attempt to refute. In my defence I shall say only that their material would otherwise have been wholly lost, drowned in the waters of Lethe: is it not preferable that they live on, even in this chimerical form? And so the resultant whole I publish here, under a title whose relevance will become clear upon reading.

Matthew Stringer,

Aberdeen, September 2020

# Inferno

The Epic of Gilgamesh, Tablet IX

# Ravenna, 1983

Mid-way through my allotted three-score-and-ten years I found myself beneath the shade of dark trees, having detoured from the direct path towards my goal. It was the spring of 1983, I was on holiday in Ravenna, and I was sheltering briefly from the sun in the Gardens of Rinaldo da Concorezzo at the *Quadrarco di Braccioforte*. Once I had cooled somewhat, I gathered myself and stepped out, turning the corner to the tomb of Dante Alighieri.

It being Good Friday, the visitors were out in number, and I was required to mingle with a crowd in order to approach Morigia's neoclassical sepulchre. As I gravitated towards the front in order to see the ancient sarcophagus and to read Canaccio's epitaph, I was jolted into the man ahead and to the left of me.

I saw that he held, tucked between his torso and right arm, a copy of a magazine. Its title, in a bold fraktur script, was 'The Leopard': it was that Aberdonian publication filled with the parochial concerns of Scotland's north-east corner, its title taken from the creatures on the city's coat of arms. My heart fell; the first fluttering of panic rose in my throat. I looked up as he turned his face towards me in reproach, and then - far worse - a broadening smile of recognition. It was a member of the University staff. Of course I had no idea of his name. And of course he recognised me from when I had at some point assisted him in the library.

"George! Fancy meeting you here! What are you up to?" boomed a voice native to one of the various southern counties of England, between which I had never learned to distinguish for the simple reason that it had never occurred to me to try. I mumbled something in a tone I hoped was sufficiently positive to accord with the minimum expectations of good manners, while noting that this year Good Friday had fallen on the first of April.

He seemed to be on the point of cheerfully telling me all the predictable details of his travels when I hissed *"Zona Dantesca!"* and cast furtive glances left and right. He paused, confused. Wordlessly locking eyes with him, I was rewarded with the bright dawn of his recognition that he was within that area where visitors are required to be respectful to the point of silence, and that others were looking at him too. My dart had found its mark: as is usual for that race, uncowed by hardship, danger, foreign climes, who once bestrode half the lands and all the seas of the globe, he was utterly defeated by the merest threat of social embarrassment. Flushing pink, he retired as I nodded my condolences. Turning back towards my goal, I smiled meekly in response to the approving glances of the Italians around me, before returning to the slow game of elbowing my way between them towards the tomb.

Some time later, having paid my respects to the Florentine, I escaped and headed northward as far as *Piazza Andrea Costa*, stopping for a fortifying espresso as I went, then turning west along *Via Camillo Benso Cavour*. I could see ahead the *Porta Adriana* at the limits of the ancient city, but before reaching it I turned north again towards the *Basilica di San Vitale*.

The church grounds were surrounded by a wrought-iron fence, the gates of entry and exit policed by uniformed staff. There was queue, a dozen or so people. I queued. I had a document obtained ahead of time which granted me free entry. While this point was not in itself disputed by the tall, crew-cut youth who checked it once I reached the head of the line, he required me to go down the street to the ticket office to have them issue me a ticket on production of this document. And so I left one queue to find another, wondering how long it had been since his application to join the *Carabinieri* was refused.

I found the ticket office, offset along the road. I queued. I presented my document to the middle-aged woman at the desk, explaining myself in broken Italian. She perused it, smiled at me, discussed it with her colleague, read it again and then returned it to me accompanied by a ticket and a *"prego."*

I returned to the first queue, which had preserved its size from before. In a few minutes I was once more before the youth, presenting him now with the ticket, which he perfunctorily inspected, tore, and returned to me. Our eyes met. He recognised me. He smiled. There was in it more than a hint of a sneer. High on the chest of his immaculate blue waistcoat was embroidered the crest of the city of Ravenna, a pine tree with a lion rampant to either side. I went through the gate.

The basilica is no basilica at all, but a squat octagonal brick drum appended with a narthex, buttresses, and an apse flanked by small chapels. The underside of the central dome is frescoed in the baroque style as, apparently, every other church in Italy. The presbytery, though, is in Byzantine mosaic, and, furthermore, in imitation of the audience chamber of the Imperial Palace in Constantinople, when the eastern empire was at its height under Justinian the Great and Theodora his empress. Not southern heat, nor the claustrophobia of crowds, nor leonine pomposity could diminish its majesty.

I proceeded to the mausoleum of Galla Placidia where the mosaics seemed, if anything, yet more magnificent, although perhaps the effect was enhanced by their proximity. That smaller space was crowded to a degree from which the heavenly wonder of the decorations could not transport me. Claustrophobia exhausted all oxygen from the air. I pushed down my panic, repeating the mantra of "*scusi*" as I strove towards the exit.

It was blocked entirely by a woman dressed in some of the least tasteful clothing I have ever seen, armed with a sort of dual perambulator crewed by twin toddlers, boys, both wailing like the damned. In response to my pleas she scowled, as though my desire to leave the crowded interior would somehow inconvenience her optimistic attempts to bring both herself and her brood, vehicle and all, inside it. It was unclear what she expected to happen if she did not give way, but for several seconds she seemed determined to wait it out.

The figure in black watching us was uncannily gaunt, beyond that which might simply be explained by the passing of years, although I saw that he must indeed have been around twice my age. He did not look ill, exactly: rather, some other process appeared to have burned all the fat from him and was drying the remaining flesh to a wooden consistency. His skin, beneath the dark brim of his fedora, had the texture of fine leather but the colour of alabaster.

"I'll take pity on you. Let's get out of here" he said, in a quiet, clear accent from the midwestern United States. I knew without an iota of doubt that I was his addressee. He stared calmly at the matriarch blocking our exit.

"Come on, move" he said to her and finally, though with staccato protestations of exasperation, she reversed herself and the pram out of the entrance. As she went I distinctly heard the discretely whispered judgement *"Romanaccia"* from one of the others in the crowd with us. The American went out and without a moment's hesitation I followed, hurrying into the bright, fresh air.

"The name's Lee. Son of St. Louis and a citizen of the world. Except Mexico," he said, and I introduced myself in return.

"Let's go," he said.

"Where?" I asked.

"Outta here. Through the gate," and he led on at a brisker pace than I had expected. I followed without further question.

He meant the Roman triumphal arch of the *Porta Adriana*, by which we escaped the tourist-bustling ancient centre of Ravenna. The *Via Maggiore* beyond it had more vehicular traffic, but also subordinate lanes set off parallel on either side, with trees lining the pavements separating them from the main road. We walked along the one on the right, beside the parked cars, beneath the awnings of the shop-fronts.

After two hundred yards, set in a three-story frontage of warm terracotta plaster arrayed with deep green awnings above cool, deep green shuttered windows, we came to the shadowed doorway of the Trattoria al Gallo. We entered. The small vestibule was cool, panelled in dark wood, the walls busily decorated with monochrome photographs of the history of the establishment and the generations of the Turicchia family who had run it for over seven decades. We were welcomed by a younger one of their number with whom Lee exchanged some brief information, whereupon a summoned waitress led us past the stairs leading to the first floor and back into the dining room.

We were early; the restaurant was empty of clientele as we made our way towards to the farther end where glass doors led on to the garden, through a decor in the *Stile Liberty*, that Italian *Art Nouveau*, crowded with detail, a recreation of a bygone age in a manner frowned upon by later tastes now themselves decades old. The chairs were of simple, elegantly curved, round-section varnished dark wood with brass fittings and cloth backs printed with floral patterns. On the tables were patterned tablecloths protected beneath white runners set as overlays between each opposing pair of place settings. Lights, shaded beneath coloured glass flowers, extended on fittings of brass tubing from mustard-plaster walls busy with paintings, art-deco advertising posters and black-and-white photographs. The floor was partly tiled, partly panelled in varnished pine. In the centre of the room, beneath a broad octagonal roof lantern framed in wood and brass, stood an island of sculpture: caryatid nudes supported a ceramic salver a yard wide, seven feet in the air and planted with flowers; around this were vases, other sculptures, more flowers, glassware, all the "genial, sensual debauche of the Baroque" of d'Annunzio.

"Old Bull Lee!" said a voice I thought was patrician New England in origin.

"Now let us honour our illustrious comrade who is returned to us!" proclaimed another, a clear, calm, genteel voice to which English was fluent but not native.

Lee raised a hand barely above waist height in a minimalist gesture of recognition as we came to the back of the restaurant, lit from the glass doors beyond which the plants of the burgeoning garden crowded together around the outside seating, overtopping the awnings. Three men were already at the table towards which we were making.

The first was well-built, bearded, the recession of his hairline emphasised by the hair being swept back over his head. His air was robust and quiet, as of one who had lived adventures rather than merely written them, and had long left behind any need to impress. "Bartleby" he said simply by way of introduction as he rose to shake my hand. "But you can call him Ishmael," said Lee drily, to which Bartleby tilted his head in mock disapprobation, then smiled as he saw some glimmer of sceptical understanding in my face.

"George Quain," I said, looking around them.

The second was taller, thin, with a long, clean-shaven face, more animated, but altogether less robust.

"Charles Dexter Ward," he said, holding out a hand, which I shook. Both he and Bartleby had New England accents, but this was the voice which had called to Lee: more urbane, perhaps.

The third did not stand. He was old and blind, his hands both resting atop a walking-stick, his head moving around as though his blank eyes might catch some glimpse of me.

"Mr. Quain? I knew your grandfather's books. I reviewed his works, and adapted one of his stories," he said in that slow, careful voice which, I recognised, had first been formed to the sounds of Spanish.

"*The Circular Ruins*: sir, I have read it," I answered.

"It has at least the virtue of brevity," he said, smiling upwards into empty air.

"My father was sufficiently flattered by your interest that I was named after you."

"It is an undeserved honour," he said gravely.

"You know this one's a *poet*," said Lee, turning to me, mock sarcasm is his voice. "A blind poet, like that old-time Limey who made a hero out of Satan, or like that real old one outta Greece who never even wrote, just remembered it all and chanted it out to that six-beat with his stick."

"It is rather inconvenient to compose in longer forms when one depends upon dictation: I have never mastered Braille," said the Argentine cheerfully. "Luckily I am not afflicted by the desire to write novels, being persuaded that if I have not set down my idea within five pages, a further five hundred are unlikely to bring clarity. Coincidentally, this aligns with my natural indolence."

The waitress returned with lunch menus and an inquiry regarding drinks, to which the blind poet replied that we would have water - "*naturale*" - and a bottle of some particular Romagna Sangiovese. There was no debate, nor any hint of dissatisfaction.

"So, have you come to join our group?" asked Charles Ward. They looked at me.

"I..."

Lee spoke up: "It's not your time anyway, is it? You've not even started, not even tried. Just read, not even turned in critic pieces like this one," casting a glance at the blind Argentine, who clearly recognised that Lee meant him, turning and smiling. "He invents books, you know, dreams them up but doesn't write them, just reviews them."

"Just like this one," Lee went on, nodding towards Charles Ward. "Ward has made a new Gnosticism out of Old Ones and Dark Ones and the things sleeping under the bottom of the sea and things too horrible to describe, but he makes his books part of a web of books going back into a lost past: now he has a network of others writing actual books in that world which came out of his mind, all these willing minions building this grand pyramid of his posterity."

"Bartleby now, well he was content to write The Great American Novel. He did it. Not much of it set in America, and most of the people in it are from somewhere else too. But there's not much doubt it's a novel, it's as American as Cervantes is Spanish, and it's great."

When the waitress returned with the drinks, I ordered some *cappelletti in brodo*, and, after some discussion in which Charles Ward tried to talk him into some shared platter of antipasti, Bartleby insisted that he would prefer not to, having a mushroom risotto while Ward settled for some veal dish. The blind Argentine ordered a steak. Lee contented himself with salad. As the waitress left he asked her for directions to what he insisted on calling the 'restroom', and followed her away from the table.

"Mr. Lee is modest: his latest project is more ambitious than any of us others have dreamed," said the Argentine presently.

"What is it?" I asked him.

"You will naturally be aware of Shakespeare's eighteenth sonnet: 'Shall I compare thee to a summer's day' and so forth? It follows the procreation sonnets, as they are called, numbered fifteen to seventeen. In those the young man is enjoined to marry and have children through whom he shall live on. But in the eighteenth the bard aspires to a different immortality.

"It is not simply the 'monument more lasting than bronze' of Horace, or Pindar before him, although this is a necessary but insufficient component of his scheme. Consider the final couplet:

> 'So long as men can breathe or eyes can see,
> So long lives this, *and this gives life to thee*.'

"His poem will, he claims, last as long as readers exist, but, in addition, this will bestow the same longevity upon the subject of his affections. 'This is how good I am,' he boasts, 'this is what my poetry can do.'

"There is still some modesty, however. Poetically he means what he says, but he does not take the final, blasphemous step to mean it literally. No such qualms or modesty restrain our colleague. He means, quite straightforwardly, to survive his bodily death by writing his soul into his final work."

He stopped, turning his head towards Lee who was returning to the table. Behind him came two waitresses with our lunch.

The food was simple but wonderful, although I can't know to what degree my impressions were biased by the enchanting surroundings and inexplicable company rather than pure culinary merit. Lee, I noticed, hardly ate, picking at salad.

"So I guess you want to know why you're here?" he asked after a few minutes.

"We, ah... he's been told the gist..." said Charles Ward.

"Oh?" Lee looked around at him.

"An outline only," said the Argentine in an avuncular, placatory manner.

"Yeah, well, so you know. You knew anyway. That's why you came to find me," Lee told me, and almost immediately I felt it to be true.

"Why this group then?" I asked. "I don't mean to offend, but..."

"This is your version of the story. You, presumably, selected us," said Bartleby.

"Some theme relating to our being from the new world, contrasting with the canonised ancients?" postulated Charles Ward.

"It is more subtle than that," said the blind Argentine. "And one of our number is missing."

"Him? I thought we'd excommunicated him. Politically unsound, a traitor. That or his bad verses," said Lee. "In Italy, decides to write an epic poem of a hundred-odd cantos. Starts with Odysseus leaving Circe, following her instructions to go to the underworld. Modernism: back to the oldest themes and the oldest stories, lifted straight from Divus' Latin. Just as predictable as his little *Duce*."

"A rebellion against conformity, the conventions of language dismantled in the service of a literary reach exceeding his grasp: we are to believe that these things meet with your disapproval?" Charles Ward exclaimed in mock incredulity.

Lee turned coldly aggressive. "I've outlived you," he said, staring at Charles Ward, "and I'll outlive you and all," he said to Bartleby. "A lifetime of junk didn't kill me, that virus the smirking bastards called the 'gay plague' didn't get me either. I'll get my three score years and more than ten, die of a respectable octogenarian heart attack, be planted in the family plot."

The appearance of the waitress to clear the table silenced them.

"We're going to have coffee out in the garden, if that is alright?" the Argentine asked her.

"We're going a different way," said Lee in that straightforward, laconic manner which brooked no argument, and led me from the quiet of the Trattoria al Gallo into the tempestuous air outside.

There was no light at all.

# Old Aberdeen, 1914

"I have been retired from medical practice for four years now, but I still keep abreast of developments, take some of the professional periodicals, involve myself in some of the gossip. This is especially so in the emerging field of psycho-analysis, where I detect coincidences between developments there and my interests in ancient mythology and religion. Understanding this latter to be your academic speciality, I thought I might prevail upon you for this interview.

"Specifically, there have been murmurings that the Viennese exponent of psycho-analysis, Dr. Sigmund Freud, theorises a division of the psychic self beyond the mere conscious and unconscious, and will soon publish his thoughts on this structure of the human mind. Meanwhile the Swiss, Carl Jung, apparently posits that our minds operate with, as it were, an ur-language of signifiers which closely resemble the characters or motifs to be found across various mythologies."

I had asked to meet with Professor Farquharson at the university one Wednesday evening of early June of 1914, some few weeks before the outbreak of the war. I had left my practise at a quarter past four to catch the Number One tram from Holburn Street all the way to upper King Street and the King's College university grounds. The Professor had finished teaching at five and had met me a quarter of an hour later at the entrance of New King's. He had bid me come with him to the 'Hermitage', and as we walked I had opened our conversation with the above explanation.

We crossed over the High Street of Old Aberdeen, passing between the towers of the Powis Gate, past the Catholic burial-ground on the site of the Snow Kirk, past the disrepair of the buildings of College Bounds, to the Fir Hill, the 'Miser's Hilly' of the ballad popular when I had been a student over four decades ago.

"I have read Frazer's *Golden Bough*…" I continued, to be interrupted by a derisive snort. I inclined my head inquisitively.

"I apologise, Dr. Cromar. It is in no way an unreasonable point of departure for such an inquiry. And I mean no respect to Dr. Frazer, who is next week to be made Knight Batchelor, no less. But by his own admission Frazer's original question was merely of an aspect of the practices of the Italian priesthood during the prehistory of the Roman Republic. That he allowed *The Golden Bough* to run wild as he did, proliferating into a grand, universal thesis to be applied to all of humankind, was, in my view, to mistake good gardening for the generation of the maximum volume of foliage.

"It is the same mistake as Marx made, extrapolating from the reliable observations made with Herr Engels on the conditions of the working class of Manchester to a theory of all aspects of history, claiming applicability not only to Europe but also, for example, China, India and Africa. The fault, I feel, is a matter of perspective: we know that Europe woke from her medieval slumbers not five hundred years ago, while the civilisation of the Pharaohs continued for millennia without feeling the need technologically to progress beyond the social state which built the wonder which is Kheops' tomb."

We were approaching the top of the Fir Hill and the octagonal building which stood there. I had never had cause to visit before. In truth its glory days were past. It had been built in the eighteenth century as a retreat, in the form of a summerhouse with an observatory above and a hidden underground chamber below. The observatory platform had now gone, replaced with a simple thatched roof topped with a louvre.

The Professor set down the wickerwork valise which he had carried up and interrogated the various pockets of his green tweed jacket until at length, and with no small triumph, he produced an iron key. This, when introduced to the lock, indeed afforded us entry. As he picked up his peculiar luggage and carried it inside he continued his exposition.

"Frazer's thesis has gained popularity through notoriety due to his inclusion of Christianity in his comparison of mythologies. But then why should we not compare the telling of the revealed truth to all the imperfect graspings towards the light of those insufficiently fortunate to have heard the gospel of Christ? It is still a species of myth, even if it happens to be true."

As he spoke, the Professor went in to a main room and lit the several gas lamps set around the walls with a Ronson Wonderlite, while I followed him in, closed the door behind me, and took in my progressively illuminated surroundings. I saw that the fading glory of the exterior continued inside: the plasterwork of the interior walls was, in places, missing parts of its intricate shell-themed ornament. The dining table and chairs were, however, in good order, and I took a seat as the Professor went on.

"I favour, however, the Cambridge Ritualists, especially the arguments of Miss Jane Ellen Harrison. The germ of her idea accords with what we know from Darwin. She builds from a simple, general idea - that ritual practice precedes theological theory - towards the demonstration of its applicability within the limited sphere of prehistoric Greek practice. Its implications are, I believe, profound, not only for our anthropological explanations of mythology, but for our vaunted habits of reasoning more generally. Miss Harrison, when compared to Frazer, treats a more valuable insight with greater thoroughness and circumspection. For this, even without the disadvantages imposed by unfair judgements of her sex, I predict that she will roundly be ignored."

"So," I interjected, "the idea is in essence that first we develop habits, and then concoct explanatory stories for why we do what we do?"

"Precisely, and moreover that this behaviour operates at the level of the group or tribe as well as that of the individual," he confirmed with a smile. "The main point is to recognise that we are not, as we have never been, the rational creatures we delude ourselves that we are. We are evolved from unreason, which in fact persists in us to an uncomfortable degree."

As he continued speaking the Professor had crouched beside a small iron stove and fed it with fuel and kindling. He paused from his thesis as he lit the fire, then, once he was satisfied that it was underway, closed the door of the stove and resumed.

"Among the consequences of this idea is a challenge to the value of the Origin Myth, on the one hand to reduce it from its prior status, on the other to recognise new value in another sense. Hesiod, for example, should be seen less as an authority on the theology of the Greeks than an example of their practice of agonistic poetic performance. So this is one point to be made. Another, which is close to my heart as well as my professional work, is to notice uncomfortable inconsistencies within Holy Scripture. What I tell you now remains unpublished, you understand: I have no interest in attracting the public outcry Frazer's work has received, no aspiration to infamy. But if we read the Bible carefully, we can detect, fossilised within Christian scripture, the evidence for earlier systems of belief, and the evolution thence towards Christianity. By this I mean not simply the new covenant of Jesus, but the gradual emergence of the belief in God the Father from an original Canaanite polytheism. Excuse me a moment..."

At this he went off into another room. The plumbing made some thumps and bangs as the Professor set a tap running. After a minute or so the pipes ceased their complaining and a further minute or two later the Professor returned with a black kettle and set it atop the stove. He resumed his monologue.

"The issue is in fact apparent in the Jewish covenant, in the First Commandment. Yahweh's demand that his chosen people have no other gods before him is quite unnecessary under monotheism, gaining sense only under henotheism: other gods are presumed to exist, such that their worship is a threat of some gravity, the issue being that Yahweh must compete with these for the devotion of his chosen people. Consider, for example verses 6 to 8 of Psalm 89:

> 'So shall the heavens praise Thy wonders, Oh Lord, Thy faithfulness also in the assembly of the holy ones.

> For who in the skies can be compared unto the Lord, who among the sons of might can be likened unto the Lord,

> A God dreaded in the great council of the holy ones, and feared of all them that are about Him?'

"That this is not monotheism is blatant. The scholars of the King James Bible recognised the problem here, transforming it in English into an 'assembly of the saints' in a Christian manner, but one quite unjustified as a translation of the Hebrew *'bene 'elim'*.

"The transition to monotheism occurs, I claim, with the Babylonian Exile. Imagine, if you will, that you are a Judean, taken off to captivity in to a foreign land with foreign gods. How are you to understand the apparent failure of Yahweh to defend first Israel and then Judah? Here one requires the logic of omnipotence: the Assyrian and the Babylonian are the instruments by which God has chose to punish his chosen people for their transgressions. Your god is concerned not only with your tribe and land, he is Lord of all Creation. Isaiah, chapter 45, verses 5 to 7 states it thus:

'I am the Lord, and there is none else, there is no God beside me: I girded thee, though thou hast not known me:

That they may know from the rising of the sun, and from the west, that there is none beside me. I am the Lord, and there is none else.

I form the light, and create darkness: I make peace, and create evil: I the Lord do all these things.'

"Note that this is a purer monotheism than Christianity has known since: evil is granted as a prerogative of the Lord, for Milton's Satan does not yet exist. Note, too, that at this time the Jews had no more hope of paradise than had Achilles: all were fated for Sheol, which is to say, in effect, Hades. But in 539 B.C. Cyrus the Great frees the Jews and they return to Judah, which will now be a client state of the Achaemenid Persian Empire. This is the empire of the Zoroastrians, with their doctrines of the duality of Ahura-mazda and Ahriman, locked in cosmic struggle until the final, apocalyptic victory of the side of the light with a resurrection and a judgement. This is all familiar, but it was not so in classical Judaism. There Yahweh must punish the generations of the children of the sinful for want of the choice between an offer of beatitude and a threat of damnation. Now this requires some apocalypse to be at hand. And in 70 A.D, with Titus' destruction of the Second Temple, that is what they got."

"This has very little to do with issues of the self," I noted in an attempt to steer his monologue back towards my inquiry.

"On the contrary, it is just here where we see the influence of the Greco-Roman mystery-cult upon Christianity, introducing a religious focus on the private self. The last ingredient required is the psychopomp to mediate between believer and creator, and so guide mortals towards an afterlife in the preferred upper realm. Observe the distance we have travelled: from the totemic god of one people amongst others, with the individual subsumed to his identification with his tribe, to individual salvation and access to eternal paradise at the side of the universally omnipotent Lord of All."

At this he brought his wickerwork case up onto the table, laid it flat, and undid the twin leather straps which held it closed. When the lid was swung open I recognised that it was a picnic hamper, containing crockery, cutlery and food. The first item out was a silver teapot, then a box of tea, a strainer, a small screw-top bottle - "milk" he noted as he set this down - and a stouter equivalent - "sugar", he confirmed. Cups and saucers followed, then small plates, various cutlery, and finally a number of brown paper parcels I presumed to contain food. While I reserved judgement on the Professor's theological arguments, I was immediately impressed by his ability to organise a picnic.

"Christ is the psychopomp figure for us. While, naturally, I make no argument against the uniquely true nature of his religion, it is nonetheless the case that in this general role he had predecessors, as the ancients groped blindly but not unreasoningly towards that truth. This is Frazer's thesis, that the agrarian cycle of vegetational rebirth holds out to humanity the offer of the afterlife, and that this was recognised not only in the Eleusinian rites of Demeter, but even as far back as the figure of Osiris for the Egyptians."

The Professor was now unwrapping the various comestibles he had brought. There were sandwiches of salmon with dill and cucumber in white bread, and others of hard cheese and boiled beetroot in brown. There was a light fruit cake and, in addition, a robust species of pie with which I was unfamiliar. He set about quartering this with a substantial knife.

"I do so love a pork pie. I inherited this passion from my mother: she was of a family of Leicester industrialists you know. Our cook does them, as they cannot be had in Scotland."

At this the kettle commenced boiling and I went to retrieve it, taking for the handle a cloth the Professor had brought with it from the scullery. Tea was made and left to brew as I took a plate with some sandwiches and a piece of the pie.

"And so we are back again in the land of the Pharaohs, beside the black soil of the fertile banks of the Nile, with a people whose religion stretched from certainly the fourth millennium B.C. to the early centuries of our own era. And this people's ideas regarding the afterlife, and their related conception of the self, are the most sophisticated of which I am aware."

"I have heard something of it," I said. "The translation of the *Papyrus of Ani* by Sir Wallis Budge of the British Museum. I have not read his work however. The pie is very good, by the way. As are the sandwiches: thank you."

"I shall pass on your compliments to Miss Cameron. As you say, that discovery, and thanks to the work of Wallis Budge, is the most illuminating text we have to date of what is generally known as the *Book of the Dead*, or sometimes, from the internal evidence, *The Book of Going Forth by Day*.

"Osiris is emphasised as psychopomp. He is, you may know, represented anthropomorphically, but with green skin identifying him as a vegetation god. His restoration to life following his death at the hands of Set his brother is in keeping with this theme, compare Adonis, Attis and *cetera* as familiar from Frazer.

"But the Egyptian soul which he guides is a thing of multiform splendour when set against the shades or souls of our traditions. Firstly there is, obviously, the physical body of the deceased. This is termed the *khat*, in effect mere meat. A distinction is to be made, one perhaps too subtle for us truly to grasp, between this and the *sāhu* or *sekhu*, which are the remains.

"Some light may perhaps be shed on this by the distinction, too, of the *sekhem*, or form. This, I think, is the psychic self-conception of the body, if you follow my meaning?"

"Perhaps, yes: I might suggest the phenomenon of persons who, having lost a limb to amputation, still report sensations, including pain, from the ghost of that member?" I offered as I poured the tea.

"I think that a most apposite observation," said the Professor. "The *âb*, or *ba*, Wallis Budge gives as the heart. You will be all too aware of the wealth of metaphorical associations our own culture still makes with an organ which is, biologically speaking, a pump. Thank you," he said, accepting a cup of tea to which he added milk only.

"The *khu*, or intellect, I think one might naively think perhaps closest to what we mean by the soul. It is depicted as a bird: I am reminded of the Holy Spirit descending as a dove. And yet the *khu* is deemed to return, reincarnated in another vessel, rather than being the self which must attempt to attain the realm of the immortal dead in the Western Lands, while both *ba* and *sekhem* are particular to the individual. We are aware, from the importance attached to mummification by the adherents of this creed, that the resurrection which they seek is in some sense of the body.

"There are two further aspects, both particular to the individual, both as yet still mysterious to me. The first is the *khaibit*, or shadow. This appears to be something like the memory of who one was. It is given separately from the *ka*, which is the double. While Osiris has the role of psychopomp as we understand it from comparison with other traditions, the *ka* operates as the individual's necessary guide through the Land of the Dead to the Western Lands."

"It seems indeed most elaborate," I agreed. "It will surely be an act of significant imagination for either Dr. Freud or Dr. Jung to construct a schema of equivalent complexity for their cartography of the human psyche."

"From what I know of the western tradition I think it a racing certainty that Dr. Freud's partitioning will be triune. Cake?" asked Professor Farquharson.

# Interzone

My eyes accustom themselves somewhat to the dark: I see that we are not in *Via Maggiore*, nor even in Ravenna.

"Come on." Lee leads, darting through narrow streets, some with walkways alongside, raised and sheltered under colonnades, but all made into boulder-fields of building-rubble, the ruins of houses still, I see, used as homes, hovel-shelters inhabited by a few animals and ghosts and ghostlike, silent people.

We come out into a piazza, the confluence of half a dozen streets. Young men flit across the darkness, whispering, shouting Italian. Several emerge from each of two medieval buildings before us in the piazza's centre. They run off down the widest, clearest street. All are carrying firearms: pistols, bolt-action rifles, submachine guns.

Then I see that the buildings from which they came continue vertically up into the night. They are towers, square-section, brick, and something is very wrong with them. I realise that both are leaning precipitously, improbably, defying gravity just as they defy whatever catastrophe has befallen this place.

I know where I am. I recognise, after the impossible gathering with whom I have just had lunch, that the issue is just that I don't know when.

Old Bull Lee is talking.

"December 1919 Malatesta returns, bringing defiance of authority to the northern cities of Italy again. The scarlet banner of rebellion is raised over factories, strikes are called, workers' councils formed by syndicalists and communists. These are the *Biennio Rossi* - the 'Two Red Years'.

"Course they all end up unemployed, and the capitalists get together with the nationalists and beget the blackshirt *Fascisti*. In 1922 Mussolini marches on Rome. The cancer metastasises across Europe until in 1940 Italy joins in the second half of the Great War. For three years they're kind of on the other side than they were in 1915.

"When the Allies come up Italy from the Med the King signs an armistice, September 1943. The Fascists become a Nazi puppet regime run out of Salo up in the lakes. The front line follows the mountains across the south edge of the plain of the Po. Bologna, with her industry, had already been bombed, but now the Germans send troops in to hold the city; seventeen days after the armistice an allied air raid catches the population unaware on a market day. A thousand die, more than that again wounded. Hundreds of buildings destroyed in the old city centre alone.

"By late autumn near half the people get out of the city. The raids carry on, over forty in the next twelve months. On the twelfth of October 1944 'Operation Pancake' drops thirteen hundred tonnes of bombs on the city. After this most of the remaining civilian population get out. Near half the buildings in the city have been destroyed or damaged. This is where we are now, a Tuesday night in November 1944."

A sudden cacophony of automatic gunfire, the light of muzzle-flash pulsates rapidly in the dark. We duck into a doorway and I wonder how we get away from this. Lee reaches into the inner pocket of his jacket, produces a revolver, steps out with the Smith and Wesson .38 special aimed in his outstretched hand, and shoots the Wehrmacht Obergefreiter through the forehead.

"The right to bear arms and the right to bare asses," he deadpans in response to my shock.

"What are we doing here?" I plead.

"The battle of the *Porta Lame*. The 7th brigade of the *Gruppi d'Azione Patriottica* against the Fascists and Nazis, one of the largest resistance actions of the European theatre," says Lee.

I consider this for a moment.

"We're right across town from the *Porta Lame*," I protest. "And anyway, that doesn't tell me why."

Along the colonnaded *Via Zamboni* from the two towers we duck left into a street which is a landslide of rubble from collapsed buildings. Keeping to the right we get past it without breaking an ankle. Beyond the pile of brick and lime where the destroyed buildings had stood are the fractured carapaces of their neighbours, obscenely displaying interiors denigrated by fire. The frontage of the ground floor is a mere black skeleton beyond which can be seen deep piles of grey ash pillowing light as down. The wrought-iron support of a shop sign still juts stubbornly into the street. Although the oval plaque is scorched black, in the faintest shadow of burned paint can still somehow be discerned the words 'Atti e Figli'.

"This mean anything to you?" asks Lee.

"What's going on? Who are you? I mean, in this... story?"

"Me? I'm the trickster. You recognise me as the trickster all right. But their dumb asses don't know the rules. They dismissed me. They forgot the trickster's the only one that can fool God. I made it to the Western Lands, and now you want to follow."

And with that we were gone, on through the shadows of the ruined city, zigzagging north of west.

Impossibly, I recalled his last novel. Impossible because it came out in '87 and I read it in, I think, '91, but I had just met him in 1983. But then I had also just met men I knew to have died in 1937 and 1891, and moreover it was now apparently 1944, so I decided to go along with it. What choice was there?

This was what the blind Argentine had meant. All the shock value of Lee's journalism of homosexuality and drug abuse, all the experimentation, the laconic impressionism drifting into cut-up technique, all the visceral expression of a personal mythology, had led up to it: a straight-faced attempt to survive bodily death.

'The road to the Western Lands is by definition the most dangerous road in the world, for it is a journey beyond Death, beyond the basic God standard of Fear and Danger. It is the most heavily guarded road in the world, for it gives access to the gift that supersedes all other gifts: Immortality.'

He had taken from the Egyptian Book of the Dead the idea of the self as heterogeneous system, dissociating upon death, rather than the simplistic notion of body and soul. And so he had recognised that one of the aspects of his self was that which existed in his books. It was, after all, the self which he had liked best. Certainly he had not treated his physical flesh as a temple, except perhaps in sacrifice to some dark goddess of degradation. But the self written into his books was the one known to the largest number of others, the self which had reported back from inside all the years lost to opiate abuse. It was, in a very real sense, more of a human being than any other of his aspects. And so, in a rite of literary magic, he transmigrated into The Western Lands in preparation for his bodily death. Apparently he is now here as my guide: apparently he believes that I am attempting the same.

I struggle to recall the Egyptian schema as we hurry through the dark, ruined streets. Hearts and shadows and doubles and remains. And Osiris to guide the spirit.

From the dark of an alley a couple come forward, seeming to move together lightly as doves through the malignant air: pity blurs my senses; I feel briefly faint before they disappear again into the shadows.

We go on through the shattered city. There is gunfire, and the flashes of explosions light the night, and sighs and cries and echoes of lamentation echo throughout the starless air. We pass civilians, an interminable train pleading in Romagnol, tongues confused, a language strained in anguish, cadences of anger, shrill outcries, raucous groans. Their faces run with blood in streaks; their blood, mixed with their tears, dripping to their feet. At that moment I seem to see the whole of Bologna crumbling into ruin, her venerable towers toppling at last from their foundations, each like an ancient ash tree high in the mountains which farmers have finally felled after blow upon blow of their heavy axes: at last it succumbs to its wounds, breaks with a dying groan and spreads its ruin along the ridge.

We come to a broader thoroughfare running north-south across our path; it must be *Via Guglielmo Marconi*. The sounds of conflict are nearer now, more of the time. As we dart across, the staccato rattle of a Beretta 38 or an MP40 shouts out that it sees us. I hear a bullet zip close past my head. We both make it over into the cosseting shadows of an alleyway leading off the western side. We go on towards *Porta Lame*. I am still unsure why.

I glance into a darkened building and see, framed in an open doorway directly opposite, a figure looking straight at me. I start in fright in time with him, then recognise the mirror for what it is. At this Lee appears beside him, aims his gun at me. Another Lee beside me fires in unison, a perfect duel. Their world explodes in unnumbered shattered shards, goes black.

"Damn *ka*," says Lee. "Come on."

We go over a wall and down into some large gardens. We shun the open ground, stick beneath the trees. Still we walk right into a group of blackshirts blocking our way. They seem less trigger-happy than the Germans, perhaps still vestigially aware that the people are their own, perhaps simply accepting that the Fascist cause is lost.

At their head is someone who looks at once utterly out of place and entirely at home in this hell. In contrast to everyone else we have seen, including ourselves, he is calm, composed, unflustered. He is uncannily tall and dressed all in a white which the filthy air seems unable to pollute. He has a face unlike any I have seen before. It is long, oval, with high cheekbones. A dark, plaited beard constrained in a web of fine golden threads protrudes several inches from the point of his chin; elsewhere he is clean-shaven to inhuman smoothness. His eyes are a striking contrast of dark irises against vivid white, surrounded again by black, apparently makeup. The nose is long, thin, straight, and narrow, in seeming contrast to the fullness of his lips. None of this, though, is noteworthy when set against the colour of his skin. He is bright green, and by this I know him.

Lee reaches into the inner pocket of his jacket, produces his revolver, steps forward with the Smith and Wesson .38 special aimed in his outstretched hand, and shoots Osiris through the forehead. He goes down just like anyone else when 147 grains of lead perforates their cranium at 900 feet per second.

"The right to bear arms and the right to bare asses," Lee deadpans in response to my shock.

The theological implications of having gunned down the God of the Afterlife are a paradoxical step too far for my mind. Something is very wrong. This is not the way to Heaven. This is the Inferno, but instead of Virgil I get an antiauthoritarian drug addict.

I know in that moment that I'm never getting out of here.

"I was never much good with rules," says Old Bull Lee. "But you gotta know the rules, you want to be free."

The air without refuge of silence

In the hell mouth, the city of Dis,

And my running form,

Shouting, whirling my arms, the quick limbs,

Howling against the evil,

Eyes rolling,

Whirling flaming cart-wheels,

My head held backwards to gaze on the evil,

As I run from it,

Towards the mountain.

# Bologna, 1910

"When the final page is turned, and the reader, having read, closes the cover, does he consider that he may be the last reader, not merely of that copy, but of that book? And yet in time it must be so for every book." Francesco Atti's sales technique was evidently a honed theatrical performance.

We were in the back of his bookshop, which is set in a side street of Bologna off *Via Zamboni*. Having recognised both my interest in antiquarian books and that I was a man of somewhat greater financial means than the students or staff of the nearby university, I was honoured with an invitation to this, the Holy of Holies for the lover of literature.

"I fear, *Dottore*, that we approach the end of an age," he went on in excellent though accented English. "The human voice may today be recorded, and Signor Marconi has given us wireless telegraphy. We have a theatre of the *cinématographe* here in Bologna now. With the pace of modern technological advance, what need will there be, a century from now, for the printed book? It may seem inconceivable to you and I, but will the book itself become as redundant as the scribe was rendered by Gutenberg's press not five centuries past, after the several millennia since first a reed pressed cuneiform into clay?

"It is rather a miracle that we have what we have from the ancients, given all the vagaries of selection and copying, the use of papyri in the embalming of mummies of the Ptolemaic or Roman periods, re-use of scraped vellum for scripture by the Byzantines, and, most grievous of all wounds to the bibliophile soul, the burning of the Library of Alexandria.

"I have here a paragon diamond rescued from that ash. It is a manuscript text of Aeschylus' *Prometheus Fire-Bearer*. It comes down to us by way of a Yemeni working in Damascus in the early 8th century, translated into English by a man of Salem who gives the Arab's name as Abdul Alhazred. This is clearly nonsensical, and may be an invention: aside from the repetition of the definite article, Al Hazred is not among the ninety-nine names of God; one would not go abroad in the streets of Damascus with such a name, even if one were an apostate to Islam. The name of the son of Massachusetts is not given.

"The text demonstrates itself to be the first play in the trilogy, before the *Prometheus Bound*, in contradiction of the listing in the Mediceus manuscript of the Laurentian library. Alas the *Prometheus Unbound* remains lost. But we now have confirmation of the overall structure, with Prometheus' crime of the theft of fire for mankind followed by the punishment of his binding, the absent third play then reconciling the Titan with a finally merciful Zeus.

"The American translator's interest in the work appears to follow from parallels drawn between the Titan's disobedience and Satan's rebellion against God in Milton's *Paradise Lost*. From the same translator and the same original Arabic source, although this time by way of an intermediate Byzantine Greek copy, I have also the *Kitab al-Azif*, compounding the diabolical associations: the year given for both translations, 1692, in the light of the town in which the work was conducted, cannot reasonably be insignificant.

"Another customer has expressed an interest in the *Prometheus* text, but has not, so far, confirmed his intent to purchase. I would have to contact him to allow him first refusal, were you interested."

I replied that I would be travelling onward the very next day, and should not like to entrust such a treasure to the international postal system. The other gentleman should have the Aeschylus, although I agreed to take the *Kitab al-Azif*.

"In that case you may be interested in a companion-piece, rumoured to have been inspired by this *Kitab al-Azif*: it is a text of the drama *Le Roi en Jaune*, a first folio in the original French. I must warn you, although I am sure that you are already aware, that it is reputed to cause madness in any who read it," Signor Atti stressed to me over his spectacles. I nonetheless agreed to take it too.

"Moving forwards only slightly in time from Aeschylus, we have here a manuscript by the Dominican friar of the early eighteenth century, Jorge de Burgos, containing two texts in Spanish, the second of which is that part of Aristotle's *Poetics* addressing the subject of comedy. The companion text is an unfinished translation into Spanish of the *Hydriotaphia, or Urne-Buriall* of the Englishman Sir Thomas Browne: this second represents to you nothing more than a

curiosity, but I should not like to impugn the integrity of the codex."
I agreed to purchase it entire for the sake of the Aristotle.

I declined some photographs taken in a monastery in Istanbul four
years previously. They were of several pages of a Byzantine gospel,
but revealed in palimpsest some fragments of the Emperor Claudius'
dictionary of Etruscan. My linguistic talents are merely amateur and I
was unlikely to devote to these materials the scholarship which they
deserved.

"Now, *dottore*, we have here the *Topographia Christiana* of Cosmas
Indicopleustes. It is a prime example of how a learned man, indeed
one famous for the breadth of his travel across the world, one
capable of acute observations unique among his contemporaries, may
yet, being blind to his own biases, lead himself to conclusions others
can clearly see to be simply false. For this man, a learned Byzantine
of the reign of Justinian, took himself off as a merchant to India, as
his appellation indicates, even as far as Ceylon. In his voyages he
recognised the problem which the Englishman Thomas Digges was
only much later to identify, which is the overheating of the heavens
in the presence of the sun, the moon and the innumerable stars.
Cosmas' proposal was water-cooling, in the manner of the radiator
system employed on automobiles. His source is the hundred-and-
forty-eighth Psalm of David, where, in addition to the angels, the
host of heaven, the heavenly bodies, the 'waters above the heavens'
are enjoined to praise of the Lord. Not, evidently, a man to allow
reason or observation to stand against a translated line of scriptural
verse, he also argued that the vault of heaven was set up over a flat
earth, in contravention of the calculations of Eratosthenes."

I had to tell Signor Atti that I had no interest in an early instance of
Olber's paradox being stumbled upon amid the anti-scientific
ramblings of one who, despite having travelled over significant
intervals of latitude, could still not recognise the evidence of his own
eyes and reason that he moved upon a curved surface. Francesco Atti
was in no way put off his stride.

"Very well; this is something a little different: a collection of letters
addressed to Cardinal Bessarion, who administered this city on behalf
of Pope Nicholas V for several years in the middle of the *quattrocento* -
you say fifteenth century, yes? They suggest to me some clandestine
justification for their having been, so far as I am aware, concealed
from the public eye. They are variously in Latin, Greek, Tuscan,

Venetan... You might see what you can make of them now that you are to be a gentleman of leisure?" I opined that this might indeed be a very interesting and absorbing challenge, and we agreed a price.

I took also a copy of the Ur-Hamlet of Thomas Kyd, intending to make a present of it to a friend, and a manuscript by Alfonso van Worden, lost until his own grandson chanced upon it at Saragossa during the Napoleonic wars. There was, in addition, a peculiarity named the *Encyclopædia of Tlön*.

As he tallied up the bill, Francesco Atti maintained his commentary, perhaps intending it as a soothing balm to the shock of the final reckoning.

"Thank you so much for giving a new home to these poor, frail elders, that they may live some few years further into their dotage. What becomes of forgotten books? Sometimes, perhaps, they have lived long enough to have spawned children: sometimes in the features of a new book can be glimpsed a fleeting reflection of some unexpected ancestor, a Grecian profile on a face native, perhaps, to Connacht. Or Caledonia," he added, smiling up at me.

"Books have been, and, for the time being, remain useful to us, and so have proliferated. But Parmenides and Heraclitus expounded their philosophies in a world without books; the wireless will soon permit direct address to a larger audience than any agora they might have dreamed, and the phonograph allows direct speech to be reproduced at will. For the music of poetry it may already be superior. In years to come shall the transmission of the voice, the moving image, or the published text become immediate, available to all, and at trivial cost?

"So it is that books today offer to their authors a dubious immortality, being a suspect vessel for carrying one's acclaim into posterity. The names of once-illustrious writers shall be knaved out of their graves, their skulls made drinking-bowls and their bones turned into pipes to delight and sport their enemies, as when mummy is made merchandise and Pharaoh is sold for balsam.

"Enough: I shall bore even myself. For the time being my little Alexandria still stands, a treasury held against the barbarians. And for the time being I still find kindred souls like you, that this our passion shall not perish from the earth. Now, may I offer you a coffee, *dottore?*"

# Purgatorio

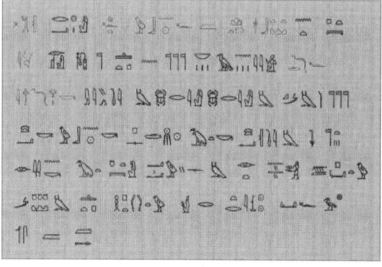

Opening of the Papyrus of Ani

# Rothiemurchus Forest, Summer 2020

It is hot. Not just hot for Scotland, or even for fifteen hundred feet above sea level in the Cairngorm National Park: this would be hot enough even for those from less boreal latitudes. The effect is significantly exacerbated by relative humidity rising towards a hundred percent. Cumulus clouds, wandering in from the southwest, are congregating in the afternoon sky above the mountains ahead. As I drive past Loch Morlich, nestled in the Rothiemurchus Forest, the carparks have overflowed onto the verges, the crowding of the shores making a mockery of pandemic social distancing guidelines.

A couple of miles farther up, located on the inside of a blind bend of the road winding up towards the ski centre, the Sugar Bowl car park is quieter: I park alongside half a dozen hatchbacks and campervans spread around its edge. Shoes are exchanged for walking boots and gaiters. Checking everything that needs to be out of the car is out, and everything that needs to be left in is in, I lock up and stow the key in the backpack pocket Not To Be Opened On The Hill: getting back to a locked vehicle to realise the key must be nestling amid the vegetation of a camp spot a dozen miles into the hills is a harsh lesson in organisational self-discipline.

I swing the backpack around my shoulders, fasten the harness belt, pick up the walking poles. The map in its waterproof cover hangs round my neck for now: I haven't walked in from here before and don't know if there are early path choices which I can get wrong. In a mile or so it'll be clear enough. It is three in the afternoon as I set off. There isn't so much as a breath of wind.

Crossing the road causes slight alarm: the cars coming up from the frustration of the traffic at Morlich are legally entitled to travel at sixty miles an hour into this corner, and, if they are ignorant of this car park and the associated pedestrians, might actually be doing that, seeing me encumbered with the backpack with all of around twenty yards to spare. There is no noise; but then how muffled would it be by the surrounding trees? Of course as I cross an SUV appears, but travelling at a circumspect speed and ready to give way to me.

On the far side of the road a made path descends diagonally across the wooded slope plunging down to the Allt Mor stream. The bridge at the bottom is robust, but narrow enough that I must give way to a family crossing towards me. As I wind across and up the opposite slope of the burn's ravine I meet several more walkers returning. It is apparent from their light attire that most of the vehicles in the car park are accounted for by people on short walks, probably no farther than the mouth of the Lairig Ghru. The heart of the Cairngorms may be empty.

From here the path becomes clear, tracking the Allt Mor upstream. It changes name several times as I pass its various confluences. Each of these requires a drop down, sacrificing several tens of feet of height, to a rock-hop crossing and a pull back up the other side. I am perhaps three quarters of an hour from the car before I reach the Chalamain Gap.

The Gap is a geometric puzzle of negotiating angular boulders slumped by rockslide from the crags on either side. It seems trivial for the first, uphill section. It cannot, after all, be that onerous, or everyone would just climb up over Creag a Chalamain which rises 300 feet or so above the crags to the right. There is indeed a faint path that way, and I can see how it would be preferable if the Gap were buried under soft spring snow. But in the height of summer this is a simple matter of stepping boulder to boulder.

As I reach the highest point I have reappraised this view somewhat: the boulders have become huge and chaotically piled, the steps larger. But this continues for only a couple of hundred yards and I am out onto a clear path over open hillside. A breeze rises as the path leads down towards the Allt Druidh stream flowing from the Lairig Ghru, that deep cleft which splits the Cairngorm massif from Deeside to Strathspey.

The path crosses the Allt Druidh where it flows out from under boulders: as with the Chalamain Gap, the steep slopes of the Lairig Ghru tend to splinter off stone in winter which jumble the narrow valley floor, especially at this northern end below the cliffs of Lurcher's Crag looming on the left. When this was a droving road apparently the men of Rothiemurchus would have to clear this northern end each spring to allow their cattle to find a way through.

Up the opposite bank is the path to Sron na Lairige, which here forms the rightward wall of the Lairig Ghru. Coming down here are the last walkers I will see, returning from Braeriach. Both left and right the slopes glower abrupt and dark against a sky still bright despite the gathering cloud.

The path follows the stream's course uphill until the flow disappears for good beneath the boulders. The sky darkens. At the first drops of rain I unbuckle the belt of my backpack's harness, but the deluge is so sudden that I am soaked before I have my jacket out and on.

The rain is like the tropical monsoon. It is not cold. There is no wind. But it comes down with weight, the bursting of a saturated sky; a force that would be impressive stood under a domestic bathroom shower. The raincover will protect the contents of the backpack, but I am sodden from now on. Hat, gloves and jacket, on and done up, just mean that I am sealed inside as I carry my pack on up over the broken ground: to the equivalent degree that the clothing keeps out the rain, it keeps in the sweat. I boil in the bag.

I had hoped, in my clearly overoptimistic reading of the forecast, that the weather would not break until I had made camp in the Garbh Coire, perhaps at the refuge hut, perhaps wherever I put up my tent. Even if I was in the tent I wanted to be beside the hut: I knew that there would be lightning, and having something taller than my metal tent pole nearby seemed prudent. I reasoned that this risk was not, in reality, very high: whether in the corrie or here in the Lairig Ghru, the ground's immediate rise of over a thousand feet steeply up on either side surely makes it unlikely for a preferred electrical path to earth to ignore these heights in favour of following the air all the way down to the valley floor? To do this and then choose me or my shelter for the last few feet seemed unduly malicious.

There is a navigational challenge now with which the map cannot help. The cloud having come down, I am walking inside it. This is not the soft infinite mist of a gentle winter whiteout. It is dark, unsettlingly so for a summer afternoon. While I can see several tens of yards ahead of me through the sheets of rain, that range is not really adequate to allow me to pick my way across and around the boulder-fields most effectively. When I am not stepping from rock to rock, the ground under me is turned to spongy marsh. The water is in my boots despite my gaiters, squelching around my feet with every step. This is where the optimism of waterproofing is undone and the older ideas show their worth: if my boots were perforated like brogues, each step would pump some of this water back out. I wonder what fraction of all the brogues being worn today in offices or rugby clubs have ever proved the worth of this design feature?

The dark blinks to brilliant light and back to gloom with a titanic bang. I am inside the thundercloud and the effect is rather different to any experience of thunder I have ever known before. I am rendered motionless by fear. Not of the lightning: if anything my belief in the protection of the mountain heights is reaffirmed. I am scared by the simple elemental volume of the noise. Even its fading rumbles sound like demolition explosions in an adjacent street. The only remotely similar experience I can recall is of being in an aeroplane flying through a thunderstorm, thrown around by turbulence, cabin lights blinking off, passengers screaming, the surging whine of jet engine turbines, and outside the anger of the sky-god. This time there is no plane. Now I am alone before the god.

At this point the car is between two and three times farther away than the Garbh Coire hut: there is nothing for it but to go on. So I do. I am not disconcerted as I make my way along, although I am alert to the challenge of most effectively finding my way into the corrie once it opens up to the right. I may be soaked, but I am not remotely cold, which is the real problem associated with being wet through. Even my feet are giving no indication of suffering from the abrasion of sodden socks. But every explosion of the thunder is briefly, viscerally terrifying. Self-control can operate between the strikes, but the effect as it occurs is a simple physical fact. The lightning's warning-flash cannot assuage it. It occurs to me to wonder how much of this sort of treatment it takes to be incapacitated by shellshock?

I go on. I find a path, follow it up to the left, crest a rise and look down on a couple of ponds sitting in the valley floor between the rockslides. These are the Pools of Dee, one of two sources of that river. I have crossed the watershed: from here the rain falling on me, running visibly across the surface of the ground all around me, will flow south then east to reach the sea at Aberdeen rather than north to the Spey and the Moray Firth.

# In Garbh Coire

As the storm-god bellows his anger down on my suppliant head I follow the path to the right to skirt around the pools. I err more towards that side, starting to contour around rightward rather than follow the centre of the Lairig Ghru downhill. I have found something to follow which might be the path into Garbh Coire, or might be a sheeptrack, or might be a collection of rain-filled divots in the slope joined up by the eye of faith peering at them through rain-distorted spectacles. It is perhaps even wetter to walk along than the vegetation to either side, but is slightly less effort. I can't get any wetter anyway.

Just as it occurs to me to wonder if the rain is easing, the dark air flashes blinding white twice in a fraction of a second and a shock of cold runs through me in time for the crash of thunder to fall. But as I stand still in the following seconds waiting for the volume to rumble away I see that it is true, the rain is easing a bit. Torrential reduced to mere downpour. I continue my boggy traverse.

About twenty minutes later I am confirmed in my faith in the vestigial path. The rain and cloud reduce to the extent that I can see Garbh Coire ahead of me and the broader southern extent of the Lairig Ghru to its left. The high conical peaks of Carn Toul and Sgor an Lochan Uaine stand tall and dark ahead against the pale grey sky, Angel's Ridge leading down to to the lip of the higher subordinate corrie from where the lochan's waterfall pours white down the black rock-face. It occurs to me that I am going to have to ford Allt a Garbh Coire to reach the hut, and that this might have just become rather more of an obstacle than would usually be the case in August. Wryly I recognise that telling myself that "I'll cross that bridge when I come to it" contains within that cliché the very essence of the problem. I squelch onwards around the shoulder of Braeriach into the corrie.

The vision fades as the mist closes in again. The rain, though lighter, proves interminable. The path deteriorates to nothing in the hummocky bog of the corrie floor, and I check the map in order to give myself the best chance of finding the hut efficiently, or perhaps at all. I know well enough that a mile in these conditions will take a long time, and seem longer. There is also the business of the stream crossing: when I reach it I decide to follow it uphill for a while, upstream of several of the minor burns joining it from either side. At length I find a pool just upstream of a natural weir, with several large boulders set across the base, back from the edge. It is perhaps nine feet wide and two feet deep, but only a foot to eighteen inches or so on top of these stones. I have my walking poles.

I introduce a first walking pole to the flow. The drag is less than I had feared. I lower a foot towards a submerged stone. I feel the rapid water pull the heat from my leg, but I am no wetter than before, and my footing is good. Second pole, second foot in, and move through the grasping current. The chance of this going wrong is minor; the consequences of it going wrong would be major. Slowly, carefully. Successfully. Up the slippery rise of the far bank and there, set on a flat high, out of danger of flooding, is the Garbh Coire Refuge Hut.

God bless the Mountain Bothies Association.

I had seen this hut two years before, when I had known nothing of its existence. I had dropped in to Garbh Coire from the plateau, having climbed over Carn Toul from the south. When I saw the quality of the little building I was astounded. Once I got back I learned that I had seen it only weeks after a party of MBA volunteers had rebuilt it, it having previously fallen into a state of significant disrepair. Were it in that state I would put up my tent. As it is I pull the bolt and crouch to bring my backpack in under the low lintel of the doorway.

When Kublai Khan surveyed what he had ordained at Xanadu he cannot have thought more highly of his abode than I do at that moment of the Garbh Coire Refuge Hut. Solid, weatherproof, insulated and, for me alone, roomy enough easily to separate sodden wet clothes from dry replacements and bedding brought out from the backpack which has been protected all this way under its impermeable, lurid green raincover. I get water on to boil on the stove outside the door as I inflate a mattress. There is even light with the door closed: the triangle above the door is here fitted with a perspex window, unlike the otherwise very similar refuge at the Fords of Avon where a head torch is required even with daylight outside. By the time I have made dinner and am settled in my sleeping bag I see that it is nearly eight in the evening. For how few miles I've covered I am tired, and deem this late enough to sleep.

It turns out that the storm god has not yet finished what he has to say.

****

The thunder abates for a few hours, then returns to startle me awake before ten p.m. The triangle above the door still glows light. A few minutes later it flickers brilliant white like a faulty fluorescent lamp. The boom of thunder follows a few seconds later. Although extremely loud, it is so much quieter than earlier; it is perhaps a couple of miles away over the summit of Macdui.

Still, it is loud enough to stop me sleeping, and this continues well into the morning hours. As I slip between waking and sleep I dream fitfully. I dream of the anger of the sky-father storm-god.

He is not quite Norse Thor, Saxon Thunor, Celtic Taranis. Where Thor is given a personality by the Eddas he is not this. He is hugely powerful, enough to shatter giants or to draw up the serpent who circles the ocean, with a thirst sufficient to drain down the surface of the seas. But he is essentially a good-natured buffoon, as quick to laughter as to anger. He does not rule the skies. That is for Odin All-Father, an altogether darker character: the bale-worker; the deceiver; the gallows-god.

The being in whom these two roles - of ultimate tyrannical patriarch and wielder of the thunderbolt - are coincident is Zeus. The arguments can be made that this is one and the same individual across the family of Indo-European mythologies, from the obvious adoption of Greek culture for a Roman Jupiter, to as far as Vedic Indra. But where they are given stories none of these others have quite the same character. The one whose anger lights up the sky through that perspex window is Zeus, Zeus *Hypatos* - Zeus Most High, Zeus *Sthenios* - Zeus the Strong, Zeus *Skotitas* - Zeus of the Darkened Sky. Zeus who, despite Kronos his father having resorted to devouring his children, had succeeded in overthrowing him and seizing control of heaven and earth. I know this beyond doubt. The reasons for his anger are less clear.

I can see that tomorrow is going to be more difficult than it might have been: insufficient sleep for my legs properly to recover; outer clothes and boots cold and soaking as soon as I put them on. I am trying to dissolve any tension in my muscles when Zeus *Astrapaois* - Zeus of the Lightning - suddenly lights up the little room like the sweep of a searchlight, and Zeus *Keraunios* - Zeus the Thunderer - tests its stability, shaking it with a roll on his Olympian kettle-drums.

I drift off again. When I wake up again it is neither in the dark nor to the crash of thunder. The light which shines above the door is dull but steady. It is morning. I put more water on to boil again, setting the stove outside the door in the mist and drizzle of a dreich day. It is six o'clock. Ten hours in the sleeping bag, some small fraction of that asleep. Hot food and half a pint of filter coffee later and I'm dressed in dry socks and underclothes, packing bedding into stuffsacks, organising the backpack. The last task before I leave the bothy is to climb into wet trousers, wet boots, jacket, hat and gloves. There's just nothing pleasant about it, although at least they're not actually cold. I clamber uncomfortably out of the hut and bolt the door before strapping on the backpack, picking up the walking poles, and setting off uphill into the mist and rain towards the hidden recesses of the farther corrie.

****

Once past Sron na Lairige, if one is coming from the north, the whole western wall of the Lairig Ghru is composed of corries. But in the triangle between the three highest peaks of the Cairngorms - Ben Macdui on the opposite side of the Lairig Ghru, Braeriach to the north and Carn Toul to the south - sits Garbh Coire, in reality a complex of several connected corries.

The main central arena is surrounded by three subordinate bowls, their floors all around three hundred feet higher than its. From the south running clockwise these are: Coire an Lochan Uaine, set below the peaks of Carn Toul and Sgor an Lochan Uaine, from which a waterfall pours down to join the Allt Garbh Coire; Garbh Choire Mor, the central extreme of the main corrie, its dark back wall composed of cliffs, gullies and buttresses, home to the most persistent snows in Scotland, the final remains of the glaciers which formed this landscape; Garbh Coire Dhiadh, into which the infant Dee pours down a waterfall from its second source on the plateau above. To the right of this last, its floor a further hundred and fifty feet higher still, is the small Coire Bhrochain whose cliffs plunge down from the peak of Braeriach. [I recognise that most readers will lack even my own nugatory expertise in Gaelic comprehension or pronunciation, and that to them the preceding sentences may read like the more noisome purulences of fantasy fiction, or indeed openly cheating at Scrabble. For those who are interested I include translations and further discussion of the issue in my endnotes.]

Had the weather been better, had I arrived drier at the shelter the night before, I had hoped to climb the Angel's Ridge to the peak of Sgor an Lochan Uaine, also called the Angel's Peak. As it is, in the wet, in squelching boots, carrying a camping pack, I will go up between the second and third corries instead. This is a relatively easy route, although a section near the top does require some mild scrambling, the use of hands as well as feet.

As I leave the hut this means following a hint of a path which keeps to the left, southern side of the main corrie, up away from the main stream and the wetter ground around it. The terrain is still less than ideal, the marshy vegetation strewn over the uneven remains of old rockfalls, a multitude of embryonic streams running between them. The mist seems to thin as I go on. As the ground before me flattens, the marshy hummocks decreasing to be replaced by jumbled rocks, the limits of my vision are no longer featureless white cloud, but the encircling cliffs of Garbh Choire Mor.

Then I see him. Up above the scree, against the dark cliffs in the farthest recesses of the corrie, left of the vestigial glacier of the Sphinx snow patch, on the sheer face of Crown Buttress, hangs the body of a man; naked, cruciform, giant. He is chained to the rock by his wrists and ankles.

Even as some part of my mind argues that this cannot conceivably be real, a second keeps my eyes fixed upon him and my feet moving me onwards towards him, while a third observes with some surprise that I have not been stunned to immobility. Seconds pass, then minutes as I trudge forwards, across the corrie floor, then up the scree and boulders, all the while reappraising the scale of the figure before me. I had immediately seen that he was inhumanly large, but the implacable reality of his size becomes steadily more emphatic with each step. I know from the map the objective scale of his setting: I estimate his height at about one hundred feet.

A great wound hangs open in the right side of his lower rib cage: the white of bone visible, sheened with a rich amber liquid which oozes in place of blood from the liver torn to gilded shreds beneath. Then, grotesquely, I see that he is alive and conscious.

# Beneath Crown Buttress

His huge head, bearded, with unkempt dark hair hanging across his face, rolls upwards from his left shoulder.

"So, you have come," I hear him say in a voice of oak. Somehow I know that, although I understand him, it is not English which he is speaking. "You have come to this far reach, to the proud-minded son of Themis."

It is him, then. The fire-thief. What do I say? I have no idea what is going on, why this is happening. But he might.

"Why are you here?" I ask

"Why ask what you already know?" he says, as our eyes meet and I feel in them the vertigo of abyssal time.

"Strength and Force confined me here at Zeus' command, by the smith-god's art, for defiance. For Zeus held humanity of no account, but wanted to annihilate the race and plant another in its stead. This project no-one contravened but me. I hunted out and stole, hidden in a hollow reed, a spark of fire which has been to humanity the teacher of every craft, a great resource. They were as infants, or dumb beasts, but I showed them all the merits of intelligence, and every craft.

"Carpentry and the raising of buildings for shelter I taught them. I showed the stars' risings and settings, the calendar of seasons, and the times of planting and of harvest. I was the first to put beasts under yokes and saddles, and discovered to men the ways of roaming the sea in vessels blown on linen wings. Metalwork and medicine and more. Numbers, that highest mental feat, I granted them, and the combining of letters, handmaid to Memory, hardworking mother of the arts. Though I invented all such contrivances for humans, in this my present wretchedness I have no clever art by which I might be free."

"I know you, Prometheus, and have heard all this: your fame has lasted through the ages because of that very craft of writing which you gave us. But I have been unclear: my question is why are you in this place; this is not the high Caucasus of Scythia?" I clarify.

"You came to find me here, to this lonely crag flanked by eternal snows, hidden from earth and heaven. You came through the storm, when you need not; you came despite the anger of Zeus. You came when a sensible or modest man would not. You came to find me."

I have to admit that this is as reasonable an explanation for why I am out in this weather as I could have come up with myself, so I accept it and go on.

"Will you tell me, why did you defy him for our sake?"

"To be weak is to be miserable, whether in action or in suffering. Tyrant Zeus wields power unlawfully. The world is not his creation, his claim is based on force alone.

"There is power in the knowledge which I gave you, which is why it was forbidden. I stopped mortals from brooding on death: I made a hope to lodge in them. I gave it that you might defy him too. I gave it because I could.

"You see me consigned to this remote, deserted rock; I am a pathetic plaything of the breezes, carrion for his eagle. Yet all is not lost, for left to me are all that I require: the unconquerable will, and the courage never to submit or yield. Let thunder stir the heavens, spasms of wild wind. Let blasts shake the earth to her roots. Let the sea's wave, surging fierce, send to turmoil the paths of the stars in heaven. He can lift up and hurl my body to Tartaros in Necessity's harsh vortex. He cannot kill me. Before the doors of time are shut I shall be free again, and he will be deposed.

"I know a secret. There is a mother whose son the Fates will make greater than his father. If Zeus begets this son upon her, he will fall, and there will be a new Prince of Heaven. Neither consent nor sexual continence are habitual to him: the seed of his undoing lies in his own unrestraint."

At that an unholy screeching tears the air. It is worse than the thunder of the day before, having the same pure physical effect on me, but also in it the shock of the unexplained. I whirl around, immediately lose my footing on the scree, and fall down the slope. The pack, fortunately, breaks my fall onto the jumbled rocks, of which a few slide away, but the slope as a whole holds firm. I clamber ungainly until I am once more the right way round, and look up.

I have seen golden eagles a few times in the mountains, from a distance. They are recognisable from their shape, but also from their great size. But the eagle which now comes down out of the damp opacity of the sky is monstrously large, concomitant with Prometheus' titanic form. Its talons seize both rock and flesh, sinking through the latter as it digs its beak deep into his gaping side. Bone snaps as it tears great gobbets of liver steaming from the wound; a waterfall of honeyed ichor flows streaming down his naked skin. His eyes screw closed, breath hisses powerfully through clenched teeth, tendons stand clear in his neck, but he makes no cry.

I, meanwhile, comport myself altogether less nobly. I reel and stagger, and the scree now gives way and slides downhill with me on top. I manage to sustain no worse damage than some bruising, but, when I stop, the grim duet above has fallen silent.

Turning, peering upwards, I see nothing but the mist. Cautiously I crawl farther up, but now there is no sign of Prometheus' massive form or the awful raptor. I call out. There is no answer. It is just as though he was never there, which on reflection seems not unreasonable, but I know that my experience was real.

There is nothing further to be done. I turn and pick my way down the unstable scree to the corrie floor. There I head for the ridge which forms the northern limit of Garbh Choire Mor, a more gradual slope than the crags of the corrie headwall. Some part of it is large boulders, inconvenient to clamber up; some part is vegetated slope, initially easier to walk up but with increasing gradient quickly becoming too slippery given the sodden conditions; between these two are areas of smaller scree, apparently the easiest climbing until it suddenly slides away beneath my step, rocks bouncing away downhill to disappear into the mist.

I collapse my walking poles and strap them to the sides of the pack. While I am stopped I finish the last of my water. This is fine: peculiarly, there is water nearby once I reach the top. Providing, that is, the top has not been supernaturally altered. I look across towards the buttress but it is invisible in the mist. I swing on the pack and continue on up.

The slope steepens and I take some care to ensure as best I can in the reduced visibility that I am following the easiest route. The grass becomes too slick, the scree too unstable. Craning my neck upward, inhibited by the large pack, I stick to the fixed rock, some of which is less fixed than I would like, all of it wetter. But after only a few minutes of this the mists thin, the gradient lessens again, and I can see, past a few yards of loose gravel, the slope suddenly end at a blue skyline. A few careful moves and I am up.

Brilliant sunshine bathes the plateau. To my right the foreground rises slightly with the gentle dome of the peak of Braeriach behind; before me a slight depression a few hundred yards across is spread over the gravelly ground; to the left the corrie's edge follows down, around and up to the Angel's sharp peak. The corrie, however, is filled with mist, stuffed white all the way back to the Lairig Ghru and the wall of Ben Macdui standing dark below the southeastern morning sun.

I stare into the blank whiteness for what seems an age, in reality probably a couple of minutes, before, for want of anything else to do, I turn to walk northward around the corrie's edge towards Braeriach. In a few minutes I come to the stream which flows through the depression in the plateau, the Dee, newborn at the wells which bubble up from the rock a hundred yards to my left, coming together to flow as a waterfall over the corrie lip into Garbh Coire Dhiadh. The water sparkles clean and clear and cold in the brilliant sunlight as I come to the bank and stop.

# The Earthly Paradise

'And out of the ground made the Lord God every tree to grow that is pleasant to the sight and good for food; the tree of life also in the midst of the garden, and the tree of the knowledge of good and evil.'

Having climbed Mount Purgatory, the pilgrim crosses the stream to attain the Earthly Paradise, which is the Garden of Eden. The soul of Beatrice admonishes the pilgrim Dante, asking how it is that he saw fit to climb the mountain: *"Come degnasti d'accedere al monte?"*

*"Tanta vergogna mi gravò la fronte [...] perchè d'amaro sent'il sapor della pietade acerba"* - "Such great shame weighed down my brow [...] because the taste of reproachful affection is bitter."

Julia gave the appearance of being not angry, just disappointed, but I could tell this wasn't really true. She was annoyed. She was annoyed because she had been worried.

A swell of sadness rose in me, moved as a toppling wave, and crashed over my joy, drenching it in guilt and regret. But then it ran down, away, and the rock of my joy stood fast above the storm, a plain rugged skerry, but solid and sure. Some marriages will have foundered, wrecked by confinement together during lockdown. Mine has been the rock which has kept me above the depths of isolation and madness.

How should we treat with each other? Plato gives the cardinal virtues as prudence, fortitude, temperance and justice. I admit that I had perhaps fallen somewhat short on prudence.

To these four have been added the three theological virtues given by Paul (in what posterity has seen fit to make the most tediously over-quoted letter ever written by human hand): faith, hope, and love. They are theological in that the focus is on faith in God and hope for the life hereafter. Even the 'love' is that between God and believer, the Greek distinguishing *agape* from *philia* or *eros*.

I have seen suggested an atheist Christianity: what dies on the cross is the tyranny of the angry patriarch deity; above us now indeed only sky. The sky-tyrant is replaced by a humbler divinity clothed in human flesh, realised in the power of communion with each other: "for where two or three are gathered together in my name, there am I in the midst of them." The new covenant is in the congregation: it is in our care for each other. Let the afterlife look after itself. Let us have life *before* death.

****

Beyond a mountain-pass lies a bay looking west over rippling silver sea to the hazy blue silhouette of high island peaks. Above is a sky of dazzling sunshine: it is midsummer, when trim-ankled Persephone plays and dances and gathers flowers, far from Hades and the baleful halls of winter grief.

In the bay is a *paradise*: a walled garden. Within these walls grows every manner of verdure. Magnolia, monk's hood and columbine, honeysuckle, poppies, red and blue, and lupin bloom in beds and bowers, perused by honey-bees. Every herb competes to impregnate the drowsy air with its special power. Fat fruits weigh down the limbs of trees and bushes. Vegetables, unruly, crowd their planted rows. And there are tended lawns, behold, the tender grass in pleasing geometry, and roses twine the lattice of the pergola.

The feast is being prepared. There are the fruits of the garden, cut and plucked and picked and gathered since dawn. There are the fruits of the sea, brought fresh from nets and pots and ropes and rocks. There are meats from the hillsides and meadows around. There are dainties in abundance, from jars and bottles and tins and wax-paper wrapping. There are breads still warm from the oven. There is a cake of three tiers. There are wines from the hillsides of far-off lands, dark and rich and light and sweet and sharp and effervescing. There is quite a lot of cheese.

The congregated guests. The ceremony. The celebration.

I gain another aspect of my self. She is my other half.

'And they were both naked, the man and his wife, and were not ashamed.'

Because they were in coronavirus lockdown, and had no video calls to make.

# Paradiso

ΟΥΤΩC ΓΑΡ ΗΓΑΠΗCΕΝ
Ο ΘΕΟC ΤΟΝ ΚΟCΜΟΝ
ΩCΤΕ ΤΟΝ ΥΙΟΝ ΤΟΝ
ΜΟΝΟΓΕΝΗ ΕΔΩΚΕΝ
ΙΝΑ ΠΑC Ο ΠΙCΤΕΥΩΝ
ΕΙC ΑΥΤΟΝ ΜΗ ΑΠΟΛΗ
ΤΑΙ ΑΛΛ ΕΧΗ ΖΩΗΝ
ΑΙΩΝΙΟΝ

John, 3:16

# Aberdeen, 2020

The funeral of George Lewis Quain was conducted at Aberdeen Crematorium on Saturday 22nd February 2020. His executors emphasised the request that I attend, and asked that I perhaps consider saying some words, despite the slightness of our acquaintance. I agreed. Julia came with me for moral support.

The crematorium, set in woods beyond Hazlehead park to the west of the city, was built in the 1970s to replace its predecessor at Kaimhill. It shows. It is by no means dilapidated, having been refurbished in 2018. But the buildings are low, oblong, in glass and light wood and white surfaces inside and out, clean and clear and neutral and utterly lifeless. Thronging with people this decor might be unclaustrophobic, but the cremation service of George Lewis Quain could in no way be so described. The handful of us who were present were isolated in the silent sterility of the chapel's vast blank space.

There were, beside Julia and me, Quain's lawyer with whom I had been dealing, plus half a dozen who had been work colleagues, and only one other, a woman perhaps in her thirties. She made no speech, did not appear to be family.

One of his fellow librarians took to the lectern. He seemed genuinely affected by George's death and I wondered why I, rather than any one of these professionals, had been chosen to deal with the contents of his library. I recalled a fragment of a conversation we had had in the living room of his flat, overrun with books and papers shelved and stacked and piled around us.

"What are you writing for?" he had asked me.

"I'm not sure," I said.

"Well, what would count as success? A publishing deal? Sales, enough that you can make a job out of this? Enough that you don't have to make a job out of this?"

"No. That's not it. If I have to turn it into what the market wants that's doing something else. It's something I don't know how to do, yet at any rate."

"Do you want a good review? By whom? Whose approval is it? You must be writing to somebody, for somebody."

"Myself?" I offered, knowing that was not it. Quain regarded me from beneath an inquisitively raised eyebrow as I waited for the revelation.

It came. I spoke. "The people I am writing to can't write a review. They are the people who have inspired me to it. They are dead."

"Yes," gravely pronounced Quain, nodding. He turned to stare, not at the wall exactly, but rather beyond it. "For the living we have speech: conversation, rhetoric, drama, poetry, song. Writing, the preservation of speech, is for the dead, and for preserving our words when we ourselves are dead. The scribal and priestly classes were synonymous for the first half of writing's history. Alongside temple accounts they wrote also inscriptions, memorials, epitaphs. The voices of the dead. And so writing is sacred magic. Hieroglyphs, runes, 'spelling', the 'grimoire' which is simply a 'grammar'."

And now Quain himself was dead, and someone was asking if I wanted to speak some words about him to the other living gathered at this ceremony of his bodily obliteration. Although I felt like a fraud, having known him so little, I had acceded for want of anyone else to speak for him, for the appalling sadness of a human life having come to this meagre end. I rose and went to the lectern.

I had spliced together some passages excerpted from Sir Thomas Browne's *Urn Burial*. I had no clear idea of Quain's religious or spiritual convictions, but felt I was on safe ground in assuming for him a high opinion of this piece of prose. There was also its applicability to his current situation. I was aware that I was in large part extending the rule that when one has nothing to say one should say nothing: in the additional eventuality that one is *required* to say something, one should quote something which sounds good without worrying too much about deeper meaning.

"The iniquity of oblivion blindly scattereth her poppy, and deals with the memory of men without distinction to merit of perpetuity... There is no antidote against the Opium of time.

"Life is a pure flame, and we live by an invisible Sun within us. A small fire sufficeth for life, great flames seemed too little after death, when men vainly affected precious pyres, and to burn like

Sardanapalus, but the wisdom of funeral Laws found the folly of prodigal blazes, and reduced undoing fires, unto the rule of sober obsequies, wherein few could be so mean as not to provide wood, pitch, a mourner, and an Urn.

"Happy are they whom privacy makes innocent, who deal so with men in this world, that they are not afraid to meet them in the next, who when they die, make no commotion among the dead.

"I knew George Quain only slightly, and that only really in respect of books. It falls now to me to put him and what mattered to him into books, to be submitted to the judgement of posterity."

I moved from the lectern through the burning silence to my seat. We watched the coffin propelled beyond the curtains. Some music played; I did not register what it was.

The urn within which his ashes were to be collected had been brought and set on a table off to our left. I considered what was to be fitted within its slight dimensions. Five feet and ten inches of height. Perhaps eleven stone, long in the torso, short of leg. A large cranium, particularly front-to-back. Apparently very poor eyesight. Poor hearing, afflicted by tinnitus. Nothing was wrong with his sense of smell or taste as such, but they simply did not connect well to his conscious experience. He had little interest in the pleasures of the flesh, and lived in a theoretical rather than a sensual world. I was given to understand that the urn, and in time the ashes, were to be taken away by the anonymous woman.

Julia and I walked out into the clear and freezing winter night and across the car park. For some reason one innocuous point of light caught my attention among the unnumbered host of heaven-ornamenting stars.

# Endnotes

## Inferno

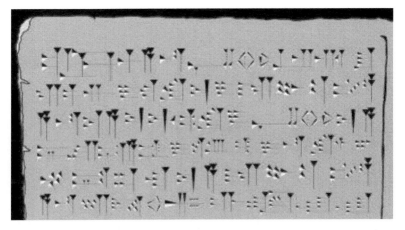

The opening of Tablet IX of the standard Babylonian recension of the *Epic of Gilgamesh*, drawing by A.B. Cromar

## Transliteration:

*ᵈGIŠ – gim – maš a – na ᵈen – ki – du ib – ri – šu / sar – piš i – bak – ki – ma i – rap – pu – ud ṣēra(edin) / a – na – ku a – mat – ma ul ki-i ᵈen – ki – du – ma – a / ni – is – sa – a – tum i – te – ru – ub ina kar – ši – ia / mu – ta ap -lah – ma a – rap – pu – ud ṣēra(edin) / a – na le – et ᵐUD – napišti(zi) mar(dumu) ᵐubara - ᵈtu – tu*

## Translation:

"For his friend Enkidu Gilgamesh / was weeping bitterly as he roamed the wild / "I shall die, and shall I not then be like Enkidu? / "Sorrow has entered my heart. / "I became afraid of death, so go roaming the wild / "To Uta-napishti, son of Ubar-tutu."

# Ravenna, 1983

"Mid-way […] towards my goal." - a paraphrase of the opening of Dante Alighieri's Divine Comedy: *Inferno*, Canto I:1-3 "Midway in our life's journey / I found I was in a dark forest / for I had strayed from the straight path." Allusions to Dante's work are strewn throughout Quain's account, both in this section and the later 'Interzone'.

"the Gardens of Rinaldo da Concorezzo" - these become the "dark forest" of the above.

"Dante's Tomb" - Dante Alighieri was famously Florentine, as Quain notes, but died in Ravenna in 1321 at the age of 56. He had been exiled from his native city since 1302 due to Guelph factional infighting.

"'The Leopard': it was that Aberdonian publication" - a magazine published in Aberdeen at that time, taking its name from the animal featured on the city's coat of arms. Here the parallel is to the leopard as the first of three beasts which Dante encounters, blocking his path upwards out of the dark.

"the University staff […] the library" - Quain was still in Dublin working at Trinity College in 1983, so his recognition by a member of the Aberdeen University staff here is anachronistic. This is a convenience to allow him the leopard reference for his desired Inferno parallel: it may be that Quain is recalling a real holiday to Ravenna after he moved to Aberdeen in 1994, transposed to 1983 to fit with the mid-life requirement imposed by Dante.

"*Zona Dantesca!*" - the area around Dante's tomb, extending along what are church grounds, is one where decorum and silence are expected.

"Basilica di San Vitale" – a late antique church, the construction of which pre-dates the reconquest of western territories by Byzantine emperor Justinian the Great. Upon the establishment of the Exarchate of Ravenna, the interior was decorated with Byzantine mosaics in the Imperial style: it is today perhaps the most famous of the Ravenna Unesco World Heritage listings for these mosaics.

"octagonal drum" - see note to 'Aberdeen, 1914'

"A lion rampant to either side" - a mechanism for Quain to notice his progress impeded for a second time, with a reference to Dante's second animal, the lion.

"A woman […] twin toddlers, boys […] *Romanaccia*" this is Dante's third beast, a she-wolf. The reference is to the she-wolf who suckled the two infant boys who were Rome's founder Romulus and his twin brother Remus.

"I'll take pity on you. Let's get out of here" - Dante only makes progress from this impasse of facing the she-wolf due to meeting the ghost of the Roman poet Virgil. Quain's version is Old Bull Lee, a pseudonym of American author William Seward Burroughs. At "around twice" Quain's age of 35, Lee is given the age Burroughs, born in 1914, would be in 1983.

"Except Mexico" - Burroughs did spend a lot of time outside the United States, but in Mexico City in 1951 he shot dead his wife, Joan Vollmer, apparently when attempting to shoot a highball glass off her head in a drunken 'William Tell act'. He initially complied with the authorities, but, when his Mexican lawyer fled due to his own legal problems, Burroughs did the same. He was convicted of homicide *in absentia*.

"Trattoria al Gallo" – founded 1909, is real, as described by Quain and, when I visited, delightful.

"octagonal light" - see note to 'Aberdeen, 1914'

"Bartleby" – from the title of *Bartleby the Scrivener* by Herman Melville, author also of *Moby Dick*, which is the work Old Bull Lee later describes as the Great American Novel. This, of course, confirms the earlier suspicion that Quain is not observing temporal realism.

"Charles Dexter Ward" – this is H.P. Lovecraft, from *The Case of Charles Dexter Ward*, one of his tales from the Cthulu mythos.

"Mr. Quain? I knew your grandfather's book" – this reference to *A Survey of the Works of Herbert Quain* identifies this as Jorge Luis Borges.

"Some theme relating […] to the canonized ancients" – Lee guiding Quain to a meeting with a group of esteemed literary forebears parallels Virgil introducing Dante to Homer, Horace, Ovid and Lucan in Limbo, the abode of the guiltless but pagan damned, located in the first circle of Hell.

"And one of our number is missing" – for the parallel to Dante's meeting, where he is made the "sixth in that high company" for writing the work in which the scene appears, another American is required. Lee's description makes it clear that this is Ezra Pound, fascist sympathizer and author of *The Cantos*, which is the work Lee disparages and Charles Ward then compares to Lee's own.

"We're going to have coffee out in the garden" / "We're going a different way" – Virgil and Dante take their leave from the other poets in the asphodel meadows.

# Old Aberdeen, 1914

"Professor Farquharson" – I have retained the change of name for this individual established by Beatrice Innes for *The Fate of the Farquharsons*.

"Some few weeks before the outbreak of the war" – the assassination of Archduke Franz Ferdinand of Austria, the act which precipitated the collapse into the Great War, occurred on the 28th of June.

"Dr. Frazer [...] who next week is to be made Knight Batchelor" – James George Frazer, most famous as the author of *The Golden Bough: A Study in Comparative Religion*, as its initial, 1890, two-volume edition was subtitled, was knighted on the 11th of June 2014.

"the wonder that is Kheops' tomb" – the great pyramid of Giza, built for Khufu, second Pharaoh of the Fourth Dynasty, in the 26th century BCE. The professor uses the Greek version of his name; Dr. Cromar spells this with a k for the Greek kappa.

"octagonal building" as the third reference to an octagonal architectural feature, it might be imagined that there is some symbolic significance to be perceived. However, I suggest that it follows rather from continuity of architectural influences: while the octagonal plan of the Byzantine church is indeed linked to the religious symbolism of its eightfold symmetry, the other two examples follow from this stylistic tradition having been established. This is supported by the three examples being distributed over two separate authors, Quain and Dr. Cromar. The decision to use the Hermitage as the location for their discussion is merely typical of the Professor.

"the Cambridge Ritualists […] Miss Jane Ellen Harrison" – taking their inspiration from Frazer, this group argued for the origins in ritual of, for example, Greek drama, with Harrison's *Prologomena to the Study of Greek Religion* and *Themis: A Study of the Social Origins of Greek Religion* especially insightful. It is noteworthy that by this time Harrison had been awarded several doctorates, yet the Professor does not refer to her the title of Doctor despite his claims to admiration of her scholarship.

"unjustified as a translation of the Hebrew *'bene 'elim'*" – 'sons of the gods' is the most literal translation.

"psychopomp" – Greek, literally 'soul guide', is the entity with responsibility for guiding the soul of the dead to the afterlife.

"Milton's Satan" – The English poet of the 17th century John Milton gave, in his epic poem *Paradise Lost*, a portrayal of Satan as the fallen angel and adversary of God which has defined the view of the character ever since.

"pork pie […] Leicester industrialists" – Melton Mowbray being in Leicestershire. *cf. The Fate of the Farquharsons.*

"*The Papyrus of Ani* […] Sir Wallis Budge" – dating to the 13th century BCE and the 19th Dynasty of the New Kingdom of ancient Egypt, this papyrus was discovered in Luxor in 1888 in the illegal antiquities trade. E.A. Wallis Budge, then Keeper of Assyrian and Egyptian Antiquities of the British Museum, managed to bring it out of Egypt by means less ethical than would be approved today, and in 1895 published a scholarly edition with illustration, transliteration, translation and discussion. It is an example of an Egyptian Book of the Dead, a scroll placed with the body of the deceased to help them in their afterlife. The alternative titles of *The Book of Coming Forth by Day* or *The Book of Going Forth By Day* are translations of names used by the ancient Egyptians for these documents.

# Interzone

The previous section of Quain's account, in 'Ravenna, 1983', demonstrated many parallels to the opening cantos of Dante's *Inferno*. In essence, once Quain and Old Bull Lee leave the Trattoria al Gallo they pass from the first to the second circles of hell where the punishments begin.

"They are towers […] leaning precipitously" – the Asinelli and Garisenda towers are symbolic of Bologna, remnants of a common medieval practice of building such towers as embodiments of prestige by wealthy burgher families.

"Malatesta returns" – this is the anarchist and revolutionary Errico Malatesta, friend to Mikhail Bakunin. He was 65 by the time of his last return to Italy in 1919, having spent most of his life in exile. He had not returned for a quiet retirement: he was arrested again in 1921, and from 1924 to 1926 published the journal *Thought and Will* under continual harassment from the Fascist authorities. He died in 1932.

".38 special" – the gun with which William Burroughs shot Joan Vollmer through the forehead in 1951.

"*Porta Lame*" – this was the north-western entrance through the walls of medieval Bologna.

"Via Zamboni" - the street which runs north-east from the two towers through Bologna's university district, the most ancient in Europe.

"Atti e Figli" – this is the bookshop visited by Doctor Alexander Blaikie Cromar in 1910 from which his account in the next section is taken, from where he brought the documents behind *The Lost Letters of Cardinal Bessarion*, and also whence came the books given by his daughter to the Professor in *The Fate of the Farquharsons*.

"The air without refuge of silence […] Towards the mountain" – *cf.* the opening of Pound's *Canto XVI*, itself paralleling Dante's *Inferno*.


# Bologna, 1910

"Aeschylus' *Prometheus Fire-Bearer*" – the Mediceus manuscript Signor Atti mentions lists the extant play *Prometheus Bound* as being first in a trilogy by the 5th century BCE Athenian tragedian Aeschylus, followed by *Prometheus Unbound* and then *Prometheus Fire-Bearer*. It would not be surprising to find that a play dealing with the crime preceded the one which described his punishment.

"Salem [...] Massachusetts [...] 1692" - the Salem witch trials, famously dramatised in Arthur Miller's *The Crucible*. The first edition of Milton's *Paradise Lost* was published in 1667

"*Kitab al-Azif* [...] *Le Roi en Jaune* [...] manuscript by [...] Jorge de Burgos [...] a manuscript by Alfonso van Worden" – these four books are those presented by Diana Cromar to Professor Farquharson in 1920 in *The Fate of The Farquharsons*.

"Emperor Claudius' dictionary of Etruscan" – none of Claudius' scholarly works survive, which are known to have included a both a dictionary of Etruscan, by his time effectively a dead language, and a history of the Etruscan people.

"*Topographia Christiana*" – Olber's paradox is the observation that, in an infinite universe, in whichever direction one looks there should eventually be a star, with the result that the night sky should be as bright as the surface of a star. The modern escape from the paradox is that the universe may be infinite, but its expansion redshifts the radiation from further sources to lower-energy wavelengths. For Cosmas Indicopleustes the universe was not infinite, so he is describing a related but different version of the problem. Dr. Cromar's lack of interest seems, rather, to be based on Cosmas having travelled, and so having been able to confirm from his own experience that the variation with latitude of the path taken by the sun through the sky is incompatible with a flat earth.

"a collection of letters addressed to Cardinal Bessarion" – these are of course the documents forming the basis of Dr. Cromar's work of translation and commentary which I have published as *The Lost Letters of Cardinal Bessarion*.

# Purgatorio

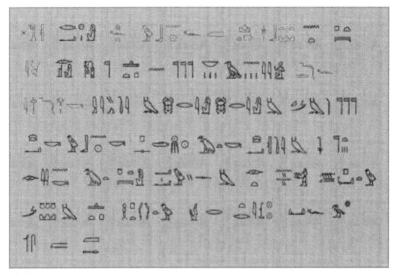

Opening of the *Papyrus of Ani*, or *The Egyptian Book of the Dead*, drawing by A.B. Cromar

## Transliteration:

*tua Rā χeft uben-f em χut abtet ent pet / an Ausar ān neter hetep en neteru nebu Ani t'et-f / dnet'-hra-k ī-θa em χepera χepera em qemam neteru / χāā-k uben-k pest mut-k χāā-θa em suten neteru / dri-nek mut Nut āāui-s em arit nini seśep-tu / Manu em hetep hept-tu Maāt er tra tā-f χu / us em maā-χeru*

## Translation:

"A hymn of praise to Ra when he riseth in the eastern part of Heaven. Behold Osiris Ani the scribe who recordeth the holy offerings of all the gods. Thou riseth, thou shinest, making bright thy mother [Nut], crowned king of the gods. [Thy] mother Nut doeth homage unto thee with both her hands. The land of Manu receiveth thee with content, and the goddess Maat embraceth thee at the two seasons. May he give splendour, and power, and triumph."

## Rothiemurchus Forest, summer 2020

The thunderstorms described were in the second week of August, the breaking of a period of high-pressure hot weather over Scotland. The resultant rainfall caused flooding sufficiently severe to cause deaths: I have in no way exaggerated the descriptions of the weather in this section.

## In Garbh Coire

The sketched map below illustrates the lobate structure of the Garbh Coire, and indicates the route taken and the main features mentioned.

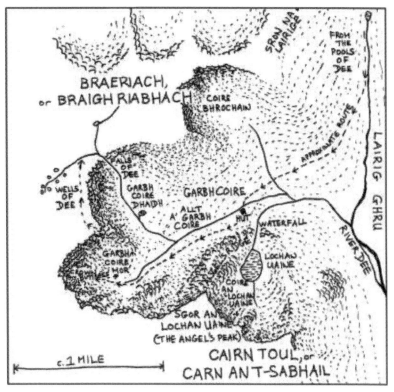

Translations of the various Gaelic names are:

Allt a' Garbh Coire: 'stream of the rough corry' (a corry or corrie is simply the anglicization of Gaelic coire, which is a *cwm* to the Welsh or a *cirque* to the French, is the amphitheatrical depression left behind at the origin of a vanished glacier. In the case of Garbh Choire Mor the glacier has arguably not quite vanished, as there are snow patches which last year-round most years, such as the Sphinx snow patch mentioned in the text).

Braeriach, anglicized from Braigh Riabhach: 'brindled (riabhach) upland (braigh)', Braeriach is not a peak as such, but simply the highest point of the Cairngorm plateau west of the Lairig Ghru.

Cairn Toul / Carn an t-Sabhail: 'cairn (pile of stones) of the hollow' / 'cairn of the barn'. Cairn Toul sits prominently above the deep hollows of corries to north and south, but with a third, small but high corrie very obvious beneath its peak when viewed from the east.

Coire Bhrochain: 'corry of gruel'; a strong candidate for the most evocative name in this list; alas, I have no further understanding

Garbh Choire Mor: 'big rough corry'; Garbh Choire Mor is a smaller part of the larger Garbh Coire, but is the main head of it rather than being a subsidiary to left or right.

Garbh Choire Dhaidh: 'end of / farthest the rough corry' as being slightly higher and less accessible than Garbh Coire Mor.

Lairig Ghru: there is some debate as to the origin of this name; I favour, with no expertise whatsoever, it being from Lairig Dhru, which would be 'pass of oozing' for the Allt Druie stream which oozes up from the rocks to flow northward to the Spey.

Lochain Uaine: 'small green lake'

Sgor an Lochain Uaine 'peak of the green lochan'; sgor is a variant spelling of sgurr which is more usually found in the west of Scotland where this shape of peak is more common.

Sron na Lairige: 'nose / point of the pass', the pass here of course being the Lairig Ghru.

# Beneath Crown Buttress

I am not going to pretend that I have quoted verbatim the conversation I had in Garbh Choire Mor with Prometheus the Titan of Greek mythology; I am not even going to insist that the conversation ever existed anywhere outside of the confines of my mind. My recollection of events is therefore the only testimony available, but I am well aware of the shortcomings of human memory.

It is apparent to me that what I have written, which represents 'best endeavours' on my part to record what I experienced at the time, contains much that paraphrases Aeschylus' *Prometheus Bound*. Other literary sources are probably represented too. Whether these are the words I heard there, on that day, because those are the words familiar to my hallucinating mind, or because in groping towards an accurate memory of my experience I have been led astray by other neural pathways, I have no way of knowing. The detail of walking and climbing I think will be pretty reliable though.

# The Earthly Paradise

"Beatrice admonishes the pilgrim Dante" – the Garden of Eden, or the Earthly Paradise, the author Dante locates at the top of Mount Purgatory as the last stage of the pilgrim Dante's journey before he enters heaven, the paradise proper. It is here where Virgil hands over as Dante's guide to Beatrice: as a pagan he cannot enter the Christian heaven.

Beatrice here is Dante's literary representation of the real Beatrice Portinari with whom he had one of the most famous unhealthy obsessions in literature and history, but who in the *Commedia* represents divine revelation. She admonishes Dante for his sinful ways, for having forgotten about her virtuous example since her death (Portinari died when both she and Dante were 25).

In my case, of course, my wife was simply upset that I had seen fit to head off alone overnight into the mountains in the worst thunderstorm of the last several years.

"Beyond a mountain pass […] in the bay is a *paradise*: a walled garden" – the derivation of the word paradise is Persian, meaning literally a walled garden. In this case the garden being referred to is at Applecross.

# Paradiso

ΟΥΤωC ΓΑ Ρ ΗΓΑΠΗCΕΝ
Ο ΘΕΟ C ΤΟΝ ΚΟCΜΟΝ
ω C Ι Ε ΤΟΝ ΥΙΟΝ ΤΟΝ
ΜΟ Ν Ο Γ ΕΝΗ ΕΔωΚΕΝ
ΙΝΑ ΠΑC Ο ΠΙCΤΕΥωΝ
ΕΙC ΑΥΤΟΝ ΜΗ ΑΠΟΛΗ
ΤΑΙ ΑΛΛ ΕΧΗ ΖωΗΝ
ΑΙωΝΙΟΝ

The *Gospel of John*, chapter 3, verse 16, drawing by A.B. Cromar after a Byzantine Gospel of the thirteenth century.

## Transliteration:

*Houtōs gar ēgapēsen ho theos ton kosmon hōste ton huion ton monogenē edōken, hina pas ho pisteuōn eis auton mē apolētai all' exe zōen aiōnion*

## Translation:

"For God so loved the world, that he gave his only begotten Son, that whosoever believed in him should not perish, but have everlasting life."

# Aberdeen, 2020

"one other, a woman perhaps in her thirties" – her identity remains a mystery to me.

That funeral in February is now receding into the past, while my relationship with George Lewis Quain has continued as I have trawled through the materials from his library. I have continued to get to know him, despite his failure physically to exist.

I recall a fragment of a conversation we had in the living-room of his flat, upstairs at No.9 College Bounds. He had paused, apparently for thought, and was standing, gazing out of the window.

"Do you believe that numbers are discovered or invented?" he asked, still looking at the roof of the opposing building.

"Why do you ask?" was my cowardly reply.

"The gulls nesting on that roof. I am counting them, but as they come and go I am unsure as to whether the one which lands is that same one which flew off a minute before. I am reminded that the issue touches upon the existence of God," he said, turning to the landslide of books strewn across his dining table. In seconds he located a slim volume, opened it, and read.

"I close my eyes and see a flock of birds. The vision lasts a second or perhaps less; I don't know how many birds I saw. Were they a definite or an indefinite number? This problem involves the question of the existence of God. If God exists, the number is definite, because how many birds I saw is known to God. If God does not exist, the number is indefinite, because nobody was able to take count. In this case, I saw fewer than ten birds (let's say) and more than one; but I did not see nine, eight, seven, six, five, four, three, or two birds. I saw a number between ten and one, but not nine, eight, seven, six, five, etc. That number, as a whole number, is inconceivable; ergo, God exists."

I now know the piece to be 'Argumentum Ornithologicum' by Borges, from his *Dreamtigers*.

"The argument depends upon the independent existence of numbers outside of the human mind," Quain resumed, closing the book. "Without that assumption the number does not exist if uncounted, so God is not required to pick up the slack, so to speak. The assumption is Platonic, of course, and so runs through the western philosophical tradition."

"But I see a herring-gull, with its angry frown and raucous argument. Then I see a flurry of wings, and decide that I see another gull, and I say to myself 'two'. But they are different entities, and my placement of them into a common set is arbitrary: I might differentiate them as adult and juvenile, I might include them with the several clouds I can see as being in the set of predominantly white things. I might count all the birds I can see, whether 'scurries' or not."

"Plato's derision of the world as it appears appealed to number and mathematics as the demonstration of a more perfect world of ideal forms. But he was not to know that it was not - could not be - perfect. We, who live after Kurt Gödel, know otherwise: mathematics cannot be made to be consistent and complete. And yet the world continues: we begin to suspect that it knows what it is doing, but that we cannot understand it. As Plato's contemporary, the Buddha, had recognised, when this inconsistency requires us to abandon belief in the reality of either the world or ourselves, the more humble path is to realise that it is the existence of the self which is illusory."

In only the second publication which I prepared - *A Letter for Maggie Cromar* - was the reference to Alexander Blaikie Cromar's experience of isolation due to quarantine imposed in response to the Spanish Flu. This paralleled the Covid-19 restrictions being enforced from that time, a disease from which it appeared that George Lewis Quain himself had died, rather before any such deaths were reflected in official UK statistics.

In time the ongoing work of preparing and publishing material left by George Quain became linked for me with the experience of lockdown, of restrictions in response to the pandemic. The parallels multiplied with the references found in *The Lost Letters of Cardinal Bessarion* to Giovanni Boccaccio's tales told in retreat from another pandemic in his *Decameron*: the Black Death.

My experience of personal challenges arising from enduring isolation are related in this publication. I have been learning to trust the man in the mirror. He persists, unlike those many selves who will not survive this year. These varied visions of myself resolve and fade.

George Lewis Quain, a man whose life never developed beyond that which he found in books. The books themselves have followed the *Encyclopaedia of Tlön* into the realm of memory, mere suggestion of their existence, and of him remain to me not even the ashes in their modest urn.

Alexander Blaikie Cromar, with his other, more practical profession; his marriage ties to Aberdeen, his love of northern Scotland, the mountains; the mysteries of megalithic circles; but, too, of Italy as the heart of a larger identification with Europe, and his grief at Europe's disunity and fragmentation. A fascination with history above all, that broadest tale of who we are, that multifaceted fiction built out of refugee relics of the vanished past, where he himself belongs.

The mysterious anima who is of the author of whimsical seafaring ballads of piracy and shipwreck.

And that imposter, the pilgrim Dante rather than the poet, that double who calls himself Matthew Stringer. Which of us is writing this?